PRAISE FOR DARRELL PITT

'I found myself laughing out loud which rarely happens.'
Sondra Kerby

'An amazing book that has all the elements
of a great whodunnit.'
Ursula Sorensen

'I'm very much looking forward to reading the next book in
the series.'
Alice Hazelbaker

'This was a fun book to read. It had me laughing
a lot throughout.'
Sandy Mill

' I look forward to future installments.'
Caley Gredig

'What an awesome book!'
Michelle

BY DARRELL PITT

The Boy from Earth
Balloon Girls
A Toaster on Mars

Teen Superheroes
Book I: Diary of a Teenage Superhero
Book II: The Doomsday Device
Book III: The Battle for Earth
Book IV: The Twisted Future
Book V: Terminal Fear
Book VI: The Invisible Weapon
Book VII: The Alpha Project

Teen Superhero Bounty Hunters
Book I: Snakebite
Book II: Fear Fight
Book III: Stormfront
Book IV: Past Shadows
Book V: One Small Step

The Steampunk Detective Adventures
Book I: The Firebird Mystery
Book II: The Secret Abyss
Book III: The Broken Sun
Book IV: The Monster Within
Book V: The Lost Sword

Rosie Ryan Cozy Mysteries
Book I: Sun, Surf and Murder
Book II: Rings, Rocks and Murder
Book III: Knives, Knots and Murder
Book IV: Flowers, Fish and Murder
Book V: Pizza, Pugs and Murder
Book VI: Aliens, Apples and Murder
Book VII: Cats, Castles and Murder

DARRELL PITT

Flowers, Fish and Murder

A ROSIE RYAN COZY MYSTERY

BOOK FOUR

KENT STREET PRESS

kentstreetpress.com

This edition published by Kent Street Press, 2025

ISBN: 978-1-923360-42-6 (paperback)

ISBN: 978-1-923360-33-4 (ebook)

A catalogue record of this book is available from the National Library of Australia.

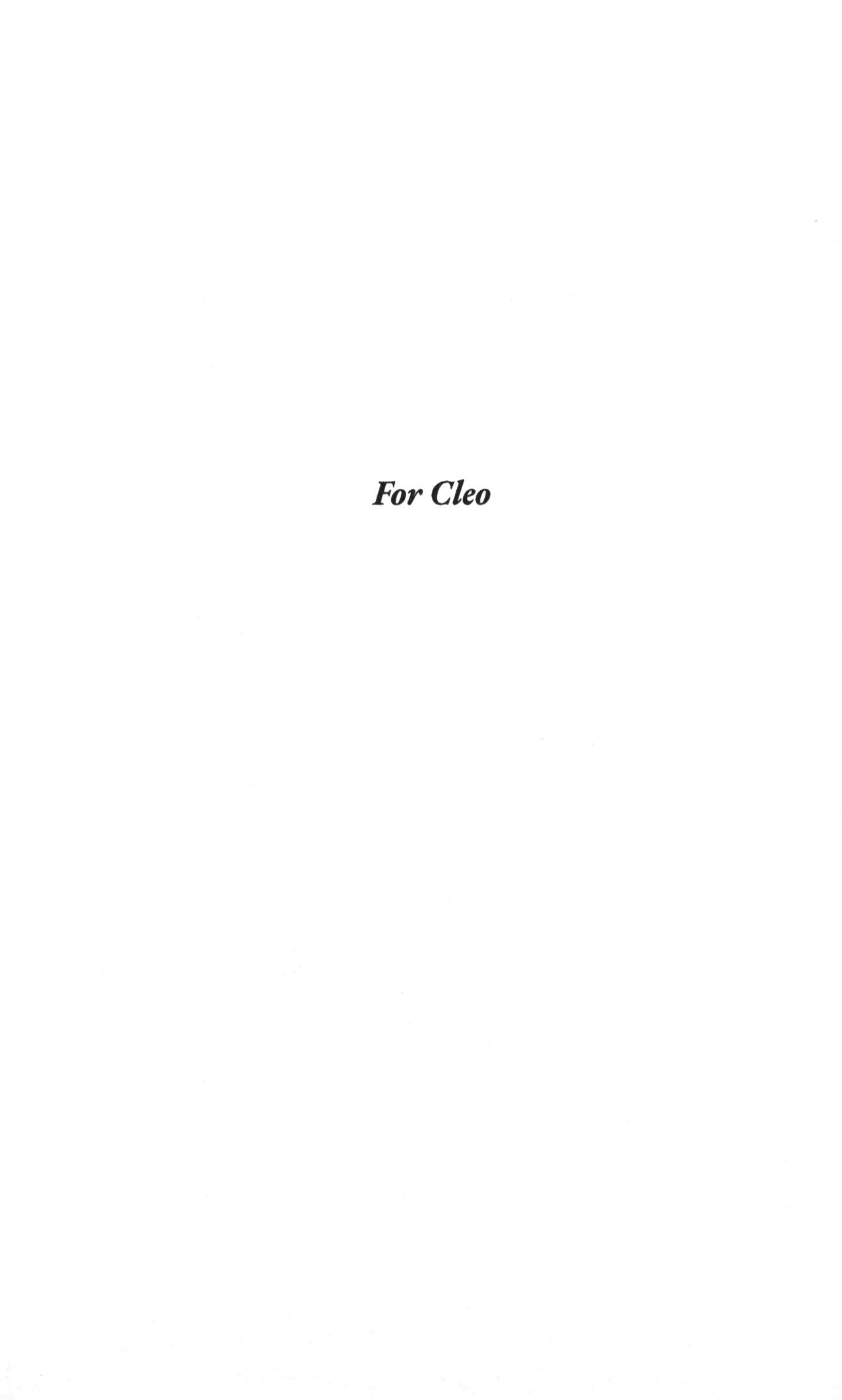

For Cleo

1

'And that,' I said triumphantly, 'is how it's done!'

Typing the last word in my story, I sat back in my chair and glanced across at Jay Patel. The young journalist had not noticed my exuberant flourish. Instead, his eyes were focused with dismay on his computer screen.

'Jay?' I said.

He looked up. 'Oh,' he said. 'Sorry, Rosie. I had some bad news. One of my mother's cousins has died.'

'Gosh, I'm sorry to hear that. Was her cousin very old?'

'Only forty-five. He was killed by a hippopotamus.'

'He was... Sorry?'

'He was killed by a hippopotamus.'

I tried to put all this together. Jay and his family were from India, and hippos were found in Africa.

'Okay,' I said uncertainly. 'A hippo.'

Jay explained. 'Aryan and his friend were on holiday in Zimbabwe when their boat capsized,' he said. 'His friend survived.

Aryan did not.'

'That's terrible. I'm sorry for your loss.'

Jay sighed. 'It could have been worse,' he said, leaning back. 'My mother comes from a large family. She has four cousins named Aryan. The one who was killed was the unlikable Aryan.'

I processed this. It's always hard to find words when someone dies. It's even more complicated when they were not liked. 'Well,' I said. 'There's that.'

Trixie, my beagle, crossed to Jay and laid her head on his knee. She could read people's feelings as well as a bird could sing. After I asked Jay to pass on my condolences, Trixie and I made our way to Harry's office at the front of the building. Harry Blackshore, the editor of the Cape Carson Gazette, was at his desk with Doris Glow, our receptionist. His office was a tiny room piled high with back issues of the newspaper. Fighting against the cloying aroma of old newspapers was the spicy scent of the Thai food they were eating from takeaway containers.

'Is that good?' I asked.

Harry nodded. 'It's from the new place on William Street,' he said. 'Very tasty.'

'Doris?' I said. 'Harry thinks *all* food is good. What do you think?'

'On this occasion, I agree with him.' The receptionist was

seventy years old and six years Harry's senior. 'This meets with my approval.'

I told them quietly about Jay's sad news, and Harry gave a thoughtful nod. 'I'll keep an eye on him,' he said. 'Death affects us all in different ways.'

As a journalist for the newspaper, I'd encountered death on more than one occasion. Despite Cape Carson being a beautiful place to live, people still got murdered here, sometimes at an alarming rate.

I glanced at my watch. 'Better get going,' I said. 'I'm meeting Kim for lunch.'

'Just one thing,' Harry said. 'I had a call from someone the other day: Charlie Holmes. He wants us to do a story about his totems.'

'Totems?'

'He's a sculptor. Charlie's totems resemble celebrities.'

'Harry,' I said suspiciously. 'Are you sure this is a story, and you're not just doing someone a favour?'

Harry did his best to look insulted but failed abysmally. 'It's a story,' he insisted. 'I'm sure his sculptures are...well...newsworthy. And get pictures. Plenty of them.'

That was Harry's mantra: pictures, pictures, pictures.

He gave me Charlie's details, and I agreed to contact him. I said a quick *cheerio* before leaving the office and heading down to Percy Street.

It was a quiet day in town. Winter was almost upon us. The air was frigid, and the sky a solid sheet of battleship grey.

The weather could go either way: the air could remain still as a photograph, or a wind could pick up, and the skies become blustery and wet. I didn't mind either.

At this time of year, tourists didn't make the long drive from Melbourne. Although we liked and appreciated visitors from out of town—they kept our businesses running—they also brought more traffic, congestion, and pollution. It was nice to have Cape Carson to ourselves.

Trixie barked furiously at a stray seagull stabbing at some chips in a garbage bin. The bird flew away, squawking.

'Silly dog,' I said and slipped her a homemade doggy snack.

Leaving Trixie outside, I entered Sandy's Diner.

The owner—Sandy Clementine—was wiping down the counter. Giving her a quick *hi*, I arrowed to a booth where Kim Chen was waiting.

Although we could not have been more physically different, Kim was my best friend. Whereas she had black hair and was barely five feet tall, my hair was brown, and I towered over her—and most people—at just over six feet.

She glanced up from her phone. 'Ah-ha,' she said. 'My sister from another mister. How was your morning?'

'Could not be better,' I said, settling opposite her. 'Giuseppe Costa put in another application to the council to develop West Beach. Thankfully, it got knocked back.' The area was a vast section of undisturbed beachfront, and the locals wanted to keep it that way. 'What's happening?'

'I've found something interesting for us to do.'

Uh oh.

Kim's idea of interesting was often quite different to mine.

'What is it?' I asked cautiously.

'Have you heard of The Spider?'

'Uh, you mean those creepy crawly insects that I chase around the house with a broom?'

She laughed. 'Yeah,' she said. 'There's those too. No, I mean the artist. The woman who called herself The Spider. Her real name is Olga Farago.'

The name was familiar, but I couldn't place it.

Kim continued. 'She recently moved to Cape Carson,' she said. 'She's starting a one-week intensive in painting and drawing. The classes are this week.'

'Oh yes,' I said, remembering. We'd been running ads for her in the paper. She'd been famous many years ago when she went under the moniker of The Spider. Back then, she was an installation artist, weaving enormous webs around famous Australian landmarks using vast lengths of nylon. 'And this interests me...how?'

'At one time, she was one of Australia's most revered artists.'

'Okay,' I said uncertainly.

'Let's go to the classes!' Kim said as if I were an idiot. 'It'll be great! We'll be a couple of Van Goghs before you know it!'

I wasn't so sure about that. Cutting my left ear while trying to trim my hair was probably the closest I'd ever come to being Van Gogh. 'I don't know,' I said. 'I'm kind of busy.'

'Doing what?'

Actually, I was busy doing nothing. Besides needing to binge the next true crime drama on Netflix, my social calendar was open. Too open, really. For a divorced woman in the prime of my life, I was feeling like an old maid.

'Can she actually paint or draw? Olga, I mean? Or does she just spin a big web around things?'

'Absolutely. She is fantastic. She was also a finalist for the Archibald prize.'

That was Australia's most prestigious portraiture prize for painting.

'I can't paint,' I pointed out. 'Or draw. Not even doodle.'

'That's why people go to art classes. So they can learn!'

'But I have no talent.'

Kim blew a raspberry. 'Talent-*smlalent*!' she said. 'Talent is overrated.'

'But I don't want to be an artist.'

'Who cares?' Kim leaned close. 'There may be men. *Hot* men. We can chat to them without appearing desperate.'

'But I'm not desperate.'

'But I am! I haven't been on a proper date in months! The last guy I went out with was that ventriloquist!'

While being a ventriloquist shouldn't disqualify anyone from dating, in Kim's case, it was a love that could never be. I'd met Tim. He was a nice guy but insisted on taking his dummy, Barney, on the date. It did not go well as Barney spent as much time talking to Kim as Tim.

'Okay,' I said grudgingly. 'I suppose it's good to try something new. And there might be nice guys there.'

Sandy came over and took our orders. Although the burgers at Sandy's Diner were to die for, I chose a sandwich and water. Calories, of late, were sticking like glue.

As we ate, I contemplated my love life. My ex-husband, George, was living with his girlfriend, Sadie. Our relationship had been friendly enough until a recent incident involving his brother, Nico, which had almost gotten me killed. Now Nico was awaiting trial, and relations had cooled between George and me.

There'd been hints of romance with Todd Parker, the local police sergeant, but that had so far led to nothing. Our jobs got in the way, and we disagreed as much as we saw eye to eye.

After finishing lunch, I paid up and ordered one of my jumbo double-shot caramel lattes. Sandy's eyebrow went up a notch. 'You know that's your third for the day?' she said.

'Who needs sleep? It's overrated.'

I said goodbye to Kim, unleashed Trixie, and we headed back to the office. The temperature had dropped while I'd been at the diner, and the air felt heavy with rain. Putting on some pace, we reached the office just as the skies opened up.

Doris was back at her desk. 'Goodness,' she said. 'It looks wild out there.'

'It is,' I assured her. 'Inside is the best place to be.'

Heading down the hallway, I glanced into Ellie Applegate's office. Our IT guru had the tiniest room in the whole building, and I suspected it had once been a broom cupboard. Still, Ellie never seemed to mind.

The dreadlocked girl looked up. 'Hey you,' she said. 'The rain's started?'

I confirmed that it had.

'I ran into Kim the other day,' she continued. 'You're doing Olga's art classes?'

'You know about that?'

'Sure. I've even tried talking Ralph into it.' Ralph was her boyfriend. 'No luck, though. He'd rather hang out with the bees than with people.'

Saying it should be fun—but not sure that it would be—I returned to my desk as my phone rang. I didn't recognise the number.

'Rosie Ryan?' a man asked.

'Speaking.'

'It's Tony Hall calling on behalf of Vivian Shelly.'

Ah-ha! I'd been leaving messages for Tony for some time. Vivian Shelly was a medium who had moved to Berrajig, a tiny place north of Cape Carson.

'Thanks for ringing back,' I said. 'I was hoping to arrange an interview with Vivian.'

'I've spoken to Vivian.' His voice was clear and measured. 'She's agreed to meet with you.'

'That's great.'

'But we expect the interview to be courteous. Vivian doesn't need publicity. She's so highly respected that she's even begun live-streaming her séances, so that people from all over the world can participate.'

'I believe you still have some people in attendance.'

'We do. Our Platinum experience allows a few people to attend in person. They also stay overnight.'

'I look forward to the interview.'

Arranging a time to meet at their home the next day, I thanked him and hung up. The conversation went around in my mind. I didn't like this kind of story. I didn't believe in any of this mumbo-jumbo mediumship. Still, I was a journalist, and an interview with Vivian Shelly was a coup because she rarely met with reporters. Vivian was the closest thing we had to a celebrity in these parts, and we couldn't be choosy.

Jay looked up from his computer. 'What was that about?'

Knowing his family had recently faced a loss, I knew I had to be careful. 'That was a guy named Tony Hall,' I said. 'His wife is a medium. She holds seances where she claims to speak to the dead and even live-streams the sessions.'

'Wow,' Jay said, nodding. 'Communicating with the dead. I wonder if they have anything interesting to say?'

2

'Good day for a drive,' I said to Trixie. 'Not!'

The rain was bucketing down as I drove to Berrajig. Bad weather had set in, and was expected to continue for days.

I didn't often come this way. Berrajig was so tiny that it didn't even have a shop. The place was another minuscule dot on the Australian map, a mixture of bush and open fields that stretched to the horizon. A few lonely cows stood about and watched me pass. Old farm silos reached skyward. Kangaroos bounced across distant paddocks.

A car sped past on the other side of the road, sending a spray of water onto my old jeep Wrangler.

'At least I won't need to wash the car,' I mumbled.

Trixie yowled.

Open fields gave way to bush, a matted jungle of acacia, eucalyptus, and ferns. Slowing down, I checked the map on my phone. I was close to the turnoff now. My eyes scanned the undergrowth.

Maybe I've already passed it.

A gap appeared, leading into a tarred driveway.

There it is.

I turned off the road. Ahead lay a gate with high stone walls that disappeared into the bush on both sides. I slowed at the entrance and hit the intercom. There was a pause before the gate wheezed open. The rain subsided to a steady drizzle as I followed the meandering driveway. I was wondering if we'd ever reach the house when the bush opened onto neatly trimmed lawn.

'Mysticism pays off,' I murmured to Trixie.

She barked.

At the end of the driveway sat a long, flat glass and steel pavilion. A yin and yang symbol of white and black pebbles was arranged in front of the house, along with some carefully placed maples. Behind the building lay a body of water. A lake, by the look of it, at least a hundred metres across.

I stopped the car. 'Boy,' I muttered. 'I knew I was in the wrong business.'

I tried to quell my unease. Mediums and people like them were con artists. They made their money by cashing in on people's pain and trauma.

Vivian Shelly had been small time until she'd weaselled her way onto a regional morning television show. One thing led to another, and she started bringing out books. The first two didn't do much, but the third had remained at the top of the bestseller list for twelve weeks. I wasn't sure if that were a sign of her talents or people's gullibility.

I had a feeling Vivian might not appreciate having a dog around. It didn't look like a dog-friendly home. The rain had stopped, so I cracked the window and told Trixie I wouldn't be long.

Goodness, I thought as I stared at the house.

The place was even more palatial at second glance. A wide strip of marble paving stones stretched the whole length of the building. Tinted windows faced the garden. I trotted to the recessed entry, feeling like a Lilliputian in Gulliver's Travels. The door was a big squarish thing the size of my bedroom wall. It was so big that knocking seemed ridiculous. *Is there a chain?* I had no idea what I was supposed to do.

How do I get in?

Just as I spotted a doorbell recessed into the timber, the door swung open almost as if by magic, and a handsome man in grey pants, white shirt and black jacket appeared. *My goodness.* He was *very* good-looking, almost like a young Cary Grant. His hair was even worn in a classic part with a side sweep. I wondered about his age. Thirty? Maybe. No older.

'Tony Hall?' I hazarded.

'You must be Rosie Ryan.' Smiling, he stuck out a hand which I shook. 'Welcome to the Lake House.'

Following him into a foyer, I cast a single glance around the interior. It was similar to the outside: simple, modern, and a tribute to the wonders of concrete and glass.

This type of house could be cold and impersonal, but the designer had cleverly applied highlights of red cedar around doors and windows to warm it up.

The foyer opened out onto a living room that faced the lake. Trees surrounded the crystal clear water, although a tiny stone building—what appeared to be a miniature church—sat nestled among the trees. If it was a church, it was the smallest I'd ever seen. It could barely fit half a dozen people.

Hallways arched off east and west from the living room. I'd thought the building was straight, but now I realised it had a slight bend, like a crescent moon. The halls seemed to run the whole length, from east to west.

Good grief. There are hotels smaller than this.

The rain had momentarily stopped, but now it began again. The droplets transformed the mirror-like lake into a mass of concentric circles.

'You've picked a good day to come,' Tony said, amused. 'Most days, it's lovely out there.'

I nodded, surprised that Tony was so affable. He seemed almost like a normal person. I wondered how he functioned in the outside world. Maybe he didn't go out a lot. It was hard imagining him spending an afternoon with the boys at the footy or carousing at the pub on a Saturday afternoon.

A shadow moved in a doorway, and Vivian emerged. She was slim and wore a long, black dress. Her hair was flat and straight and reached down to her waist. I'd seen her picture before, but she was more imposing in person.

Her fingers were studded with an assortment of rings: red, blue, orange, green. This was nothing compared to the necklace. It had so many colours it was like she was wearing a rainbow.

They're all fake, I thought.

I remembered reading an interview where Vivian spoke about buying costume jewellery because she loved the colours. None of it was ever worth anything. She wore it to add some splash to her appearance.

'Rosie,' Vivian strode over and firmly shook my hand. 'So pleased to meet you.'

'Likewise. This is a beautiful home.'

'Thank you. Life has been kind.'

Being a criminal hasn't hurt either.

Vivian continued. 'You've already met my husband, Tony.'

'I have.' I glanced back at him. Maybe I was imagining things, but she looked to be about forty. That put a ten-year age gap between Vivian and her husband. 'Have you lived here long?'

'We built the house. There had been another building here:

an old, falling-down farmhouse. The lake was here too, although it was a mess. We had it cleaned out and deepened.'

I nodded to the tiny building nestled amongst the trees. 'Is that a church?'

'A chapel.' It was Tony who answered. 'Vivian uses it to enhance her psychic vibration.'

I'm sure she does.

They motioned me to a leather lounge chair. I sat down, and it was so soft that I was almost swallowed whole. Tony went to get us cold drinks while I got out my notebook.

'This is a huge house,' I said. 'Is it only yourself and Tony here?'

'We have a chef who comes in occasionally. Neither Tony nor I are the best cooks. A cleaner visits once a week. So do the gardeners.'

'It seems peaceful here.'

'Peace and quiet are conducive to connecting with the spirit world.'

'I see.' My eyes angled over to a slim bookcase. I struggled out of the lounge chair and crossed to it. The books were by Vivian: *The Other Side, Love Everlasting, Together Though Parted, Making Contact,* and others. She'd been busy. 'You're quite prolific.'

'A lot of people have wanted to know about my work.'

Tony arrived with a jug and some glasses. 'We rarely give

interviews,' he said. 'As I mentioned on the phone, these days Vivian prefers to hold private sessions for small groups.'

'And there's the live-streaming,' I added.

He nodded. 'The live-streaming lets Vivian connect with a global audience,' he explained. 'Sometimes the spirits have messages for those who can't physically be here for the Platinum experience.'

'The Platinum experience is a traditional séance?'

'If there is such a thing,' Vivian said, smiling. 'Every séance is different depending on the spirits who wish to make contact.'

I wondered why I'd been invited here. Vivian obviously had a lot of money. Maybe she had a new book coming out. Celebrities—even questionable ones like Vivian Shelly—only contacted the media when they wanted something.

'There's a lot of interest in the psychic world,' Vivian continued. 'People sometimes have misconceptions.' She nodded to her husband. 'Although Tony grew up in this area, I'm a stranger. I grew up in far-north Queensland. We're hoping to allay people's concerns about me.'

Misconceptions? And concerns?

What did she mean?

'What makes you think people are concerned?' I asked carefully.

Vivian and Tony exchanged glances.

'We've received a few nasty parcels,' Tony said. 'They're

from idiots who don't know anything—'

Vivian tut-tutted him. 'That's why Rosie's here,' she said. 'To set the record straight.'

Actually, I thought. *That isn't why Rosie's here. I'm here to get a story for the paper.*

It didn't surprise me that Vivian had been targeted.

People had differing opinions about mediums and contacting the dead.

'I'm happy to tell your side of the story,' I said.

'Have you read any of Vivian's books?' Tony asked.

I said I hadn't.

'I can briefly tell you my story,' Vivian said. 'Then you can ask me any other questions to fill in the gaps.' She paused. 'It began when I was a child. My grandfather lived with us. He was old and unwell. I adored him. One morning, I went in to see him, but he'd passed on to the next world. Of course, I didn't know. I was only seven.'

'I see.'

'A few days after that, I began to feel his presence. It was as if he were still there. He had a shuffling gait, and I could almost hear him walking around the house. Sometimes I even felt like he was standing beside me. I'd look up, expecting to see him, but there was no one there.

'One night, I lay in bed and focused on him. After a few minutes, I picked up some words and phrases. His voice said he'd moved onto the spirit realm, but he was fine and happy. He was there with my grandmother. There was nothing to fear. The spirit realm was beyond the curtain. He said we would all be together again one day.

'After that, I didn't feel so lonely or afraid. His presence slowly left me over the following weeks, and I thought no more about it. It wasn't until I was an adult that I remembered back to what had happened. At that time, a friend was killed in an accident, and I was upset about her passing.

'Suddenly, out of nowhere, I felt her presence. It was as if she were sitting in the room with me. I spoke to her, and I could hear her words in my mind. She wanted me to tell her parents she was fine. I said her parents wouldn't believe that I had spoken to her. She said to mention their cat, Billie. She said she was with Billie in the spirit world because our pets go there too.'

There was something in the way Vivian spoke that had me mesmerised. Now I gathered myself and quickly scribbled notes. 'So,' I said. 'What did you tell her parents?'

'I was quite nervous.' Vivian gave an embarrassed laugh. 'I thought they would throw me out of their house. At first, they were polite when I told them I'd felt their daughter's presence. They thought I might have been imagining it. Then I mentioned their cat, and they knew I'd experienced something special.

'You see, the cat had died years before I'd met them. It was when their daughter was only a baby. There was no way she would even remember the cat and no way I could know about it.'

'Okay,' I said, nodding. 'So, how did you make the transition to becoming a professional medium?'

Tony cut in. 'We don't really like that term professional medium,' he said. 'That makes it sound like a business. We prefer either, just medium, or clairvoyant.'

I thought about the books on the shelves, the Platinum experience, and the live-streaming. It certainly looked like a business. But I simply nodded.

'Soon after,' Vivian continued, 'a friend asked me to do a reading at their house. Although I only expected a few people, about a dozen turned up. That was my first séance. I helped make connections between a few of them and some loved ones who had passed. That led to a booking at a local hotel.'

She explained that the first booking had led to a second and a third. Soon, she was appearing at a venue every week. A television appearance had brought her attention all around the country.

Vivian had come a long way in a short time. Of course, all that meant to me was that she'd been a successful business-woman. And she'd done it in a disreputable fashion; she'd lied to people about being able to speak to the dead.

'So the Platinum experience is limited to only a few people?' I said.

'No more than half a dozen. I don't like travelling anymore. It's tiring. And, besides, I can help more people using the wonders of live-streaming.'

I thought of all those people plugging in to be part of the séance. It could be dozens. Hundreds. Maybe even thousands. Even at a few bucks a pop, it could be a massive money earner.

'Vivian,' Tony said. 'Why don't we show Rosie the Scarlet Room?'

The Scarlet Room? I thought. *Sounds like something out of a horror film.*

The medium agreed, and I followed her and Tony down the hall to an open doorway on the left. A circular table sat in the middle, and two television screens faced each other on opposite walls. Besides them, everything else was scarlet: the walls, ceiling, chairs, floor, and table.

'It's certainly very...er, scarlet,' I said.

'The colour helps to channel my energies,' Vivian said.

'I see,' I said, although it sounded like more gobbledygook. 'And the televisions?'

'The group assembles here,' Tony explained. 'We transmit our energies to Vivian in the chapel. We can view Vivian on one screen and see the numbers from the live-streaming feed on the other.'

I frowned. 'So Vivian runs the séance from the chapel?'

'The Scarlet room and the chapel are on the same ley line.'

'Oh, I see.'

This is awful, I thought. *And you're charging people money for this.*

I looked more closely. A small console was set flush into the wood, presumably where Tony would be sitting. From there he could control the television and chapel camera. The table surface was inlaid with ancient symbols.

'Vivian,' I said. 'What do these mean?'

'They're runes. An ancient Scandinavian language, they date back almost two thousand years. Most of these represent life, death, and the eternal wheel.'

We continued down the hall to a door at the end of the house. The rain had stopped, leaving the footpath and grass saturated. The sound of dripping water from the surrounding trees was like the pitter-patter of tiny feet as we followed the path around the lake to the chapel. The little building was nestled in among the trees. While you could see it from the living room, it was almost invisible from the path until you were almost on it. Although there were small churches all around Australia, this was the tiniest I'd ever seen.

'We had the chapel imported from Shropshire in England,' Tony explained. 'It dates back to the fifteen hundreds.'

Although the roof looked new, the stonework was old, and

the oak door looked ancient. Tony pushed it open. I peered into a windowless room that was about six feet square with another smaller door at the back. In the middle sat a table and a chair.

'My goodness,' I said, unsure what else I could say. Not only was it hard to believe that she'd been allowed to move the chapel to Australia, but that she could afford the expense. It must have cost a fortune. The room was so tiny that you couldn't fit a pew in here. Or an altar. And without windows, it was a cold, dry room. I couldn't see how this could have ever been a chapel. 'And this helps you to...'

'Channel my psychic energies,' Vivian said. She pointed to a camera over the door that was aimed at the chair. 'This transmits back to the live feed.'

'Okay.'

I tried to keep my face impassive. The whole thing was cuckoo. Judging by the expression on Tony's face, he believed everything she was saying.

Or he was as good an actor as Vivian.

We continued around the lake path back to the house and in through the opposite end. The first room leading off the hall was a dedicated technology room. The console in there looked like it could have sent man to the moon. Dozens of controls appeared to run a sound system for the house as well as air conditioning and IT systems. Continuing on, we passed by several small bedrooms. This place was huge; it could house a dozen people.

By the time we reached the living room, an idea had begun to brew in my mind.

'Although the sessions are live-streamed,' I said, 'it would be interesting for people to know what it's like from a participant's perspective.' I paused, thinking about Kim. 'If I could attend, I'd bring a photographer with me too.'

Kim wasn't a photographer, but she had a keen interest in anything to do with the paranormal.

Tony was shaking his head. 'We don't allow reporters to attend our sessions—'

Vivian held up a hand. 'Don't be so quick to judge,' she said. 'Thousands of people are watching from home. To have someone write a report would make people feel even more like they're part of the event.'

'I would be fair in my coverage of what I observe,' I added. 'And we wouldn't take photos of the participants without their permission.'

'So many people have been misinformed about mediums.' Vivian smiled. 'Our next session is tomorrow evening. We'd need to check with the attendees. You and your photographer can attend if they agree.'

Tony said he would ring and let me know. After thanking Vivian again, I was led back to my car by Tony. Trixie barked excitedly as I climbed in, started the engine, and wound down the window.

'You're very fortunate,' Tony said. 'Vivian hasn't agreed to a journalist attending one of her sessions for years.'

'It should make for an interesting night.'

'More than interesting. You'll get an insight into what lies beyond the grave.'

I smiled and nodded, but I was thinking *I'll believe it when I see it.*

3

Stomping into the living room, I threw my bag on the lounge and plopped down beside it.

'I'm exhausted,' I declared.

My grandmother—Nan, to everyone who knew her—was sitting at the dining room table.

She glanced up from her knitting. Her latest project, with the local Zonta Club, involved knitting clothing for premature babies. The outfits were due to be donated to the hospital at the end of the month. 'Big day?' she asked.

I told her about driving out to see Vivian and her husband.

'Mediums,' Nan said thoughtfully. 'My mother thought she was sensitive.'

'Really?'

'This was your great grandmother, Adelaide. She even worked as a medium for a while. I don't know if there was any truth in it or if she was kidding herself.' Nan paused. 'Mind you, I sometimes feel Frank's presence.'

Frank had been her husband. 'I didn't know that.'

'Rosie, it could be an old lady's imagination—or he could be visiting me from time to time. What do you think?'

'I'm not sure.' I didn't want to hurt my grandmother. I also didn't want to lie to her. 'Would the dead really want to contact us?'

Nan shrugged. 'I don't know, Rosie,' she said. 'I suppose we'll eventually know what's on the other side—some of us sooner than others.'

I laughed. 'Nan,' I said. 'You'll live forever.'

'Hey! I'm not going anywhere! I'm talking about all those old people. I'm living to be a hundred. After that, I'm taking it one decade at a time.'

Shaking my head, I told her I was taking Trixie for a walk to Cut Rock. Soon, I was following the trail through our nearby bushland. It only took a few minutes to reach the cliff overlooking the ocean. It was late in the day, though quite a crowd had gathered. They were peering out at the sea, some with binoculars. I had a pretty good idea of what was going on.

Storms had come and gone during the day. Now the sky was darkening over the heaving ocean with the brisk onshore breeze turning the tips of the waves silver.

A man cried out and pointed. 'There!' he yelled.

Against the roiling ocean, a dark shape emerged a few hundred metres offshore and cast a spray of white foam into the air.

Trixie gave an excited bark as she stared out at the water. I lifted her up so she could see what lay out there.

'It's whale season,' I murmured softly to her. 'There'll be lots of whales over the next few months.'

Whales usually passed this section of coast from June to September, but they'd started early this year. Despite the distance between the whales and the shore, it never failed to excite me. I loved the thought of their vast shapes moving under the silent water as they followed the same invisible path their ancestors had taken for thousands of years.

A few people were taking pictures and videos. Others chatted excitedly. One man strolled over and leaned on the fence beside me.

'That's quite a sight,' he said.

'It's pretty amazing,' I admitted, putting Trixie down.

'You're a local?' he asked. 'You must get used to whales.'

I looked at him more closely. He was a little younger than me, tallish, with a long batch of unruly red hair. His face was lean with a strong jaw, reminiscent of an ancient Greek statue. Although I tried not to stare, it wasn't easy.

'Some things you never get used to,' I said. 'I love whales. They're huge animals, and you only catch a glimpse.' The whale broke the surface again. 'A lot remains hidden.'

The man gave an easy laugh. 'People are like that too.'

'But less trustworthy,' I said.

He nodded. 'Sometimes.'

Smiling, I wished him a good evening and tried to saunter away casually. Unfortunately, my foot caught on Trixie's leash, and I fell. The man strode over and helped me up, his hand on my arm firm yet gentle.

Before I could make even more of a fool of myself, I wished him goodnight again and escaped down the bush track back towards home.

'Trixie,' I said when he was out of sight. 'He was hot.'

She whined.

'You noticed too?' I said, grinning. 'You are such a *smart* dog.'

Soon, I was back home and found Nan had cooked dinner.

She'd thrown together a mushroom risotto, one of her many specialties. We sat and ate. I had just finished when my phone rang: Kim.

'I've got exciting news!' she gushed. 'We're booked in for art classes!'

'Oh great,' I said without enthusiasm. 'This is with Insect Woman?'

'The Spider! Olga Farago!'

I sighed. 'Can't we just paint by numbers?' I asked. 'You can do those classes with champagne and chocolates.'

'You can't create great artworks when you're drunk!'

'It didn't stop Picasso.'

'But have you seen his paintings? His women all have upside-down faces. That's what drunk painting gets you!'

I told Kim about the meeting with Vivian Shelly and Tony Hall.

'Wow,' Kim said. 'A séance. That's cool. I've told you about my Aunt Alice.'

'Only about a million times. She could see the future but not the truck that ran her over. Anyway, I'll talk to you later. I'm going to hunker down to some mindless TV.'

'Are you kidding? Mystery Book Club's on tonight.'

I cursed. 'I forgot all about it,' I said. 'What book is it?'

'*Who Killed Thelma Thipps?*'

'I'm not feeling well.'

'Liar!'

'Oh! All right! I'll see you at the meeting!'

Grumbling, I sat back on the lounge as Nan grinned. 'Haven't read the book?' she said. 'That's not like you.'

It was exactly like me, and Nan knew it!

Minutes later, I was stumbling in the front entrance of the Cape Carson library. It was a large building with a curving glass front, timber panels, and an open layout. Manoeuvring around the shelves, I went to one of the library's many meeting rooms where the meeting had already started. A sea of faces looked up as I entered.

'Better late than never!' Wanda Gibson boomed.

Apologising, I slid into a seat beside Kim and pulled out my copy of the book. The usual crowd had turned up: a big jolly woman named Marlene Hogan, the elderly twins, Nola and Monica Evans, Daisy Butler from the newsagency, and Edward Blayney from the bakery. The final member to complete the group was Doris from my office.

It seemed they were already in mid-discussion about the book. Although Wanda was pleased with it, Marlene wasn't so taken.

'But it's always the husband,' she complained. 'Why does it always have to be the husband?'

'I agree,' Edward said. 'My wife and I have been married for twenty years, and I haven't had a murderous thought about her.'

'She'd be happy to hear that,' I said.

'It's true, though,' Daisy said. She was the youngest of the group. 'Why are husbands always plotting to kill their wives? It would never be the other way around.'

Kim sighed. 'You've obviously never been married,' she said. 'I've had murderous thoughts about Robert.' Like me, Kim was divorced. 'I mean, not *serious* thoughts. I haven't hired a hitman.'

Nola Evans was nodding vigorously. 'I think we all have

murderous thoughts sometimes,' she said. 'Sisters can also be *so* painful.'

'Speak for yourself!' Monica snapped.

I sighed. 'Are you two fighting again?'

'We're always arguing over the television!' Nola said.

'She wants to watch Midsomer Murders—' Monica said.

'—while I want to see Morse!' Nola said.

'Can't you just buy a second TV?' Kim asked.

'Oh no,' Monica said. 'We love watching TV together.'

Wanda Gibson snorted. 'Can we return to the book?' she said. 'That clue on page twenty-two was far too obvious.'

Much of the remaining meeting was spent discussing the clue Wanda had spotted, but everyone else had blithely skipped over, not realising that a barbeque chicken was a perfect place to hide a murder weapon. After the meeting wrapped up, I stood chatting to Kim and Wanda while we drank tea and sampled Edward's tarts from his shop.

'Goodness,' Wanda said, wolfing down the tasty treat. 'Ed's outdone himself this time.'

'I know,' I said dismally. I was already on my third tart, and it looked like another was on the cards. I told Wanda I might attend one of Vivian Shelly's séances.

Wanda snorted. 'Mediums!' she said. 'Hogwash.'

'So you don't believe in them?'

'I don't believe in anything I can't see, hear, taste, feel or smell,' Wanda said. 'Psychic phenomenon is as real as flying saucers and ghosts.'

She didn't believe in those either.

'You said Vivian Shelly's husband is Tony Hall?' Kim said, frowning. 'Shona from the library went to school with him. She might have some interesting background.'

The meeting was breaking up now, and I'd be having my stomach pumped if I ate more of Ed's magnificent tarts. Saying goodnight to everyone, Kim and I headed into the library to find Shona. She was a skinny woman with a big mop of black hair who usually worked evenings.

'Tony Hall?' she said when we asked her. 'Sure, I went to school with him. He was the hottest guy in our year. I heard he got married to that awful woman.'

I shot a sideways glance at Kim. 'Why do you call her that?'

'Because she broke up a perfectly good relationship. Tony and another girl from school, Melissa Martin, were childhood sweethearts. They dated at high school before leaving for Melbourne, where they went to university together. He got a science degree. She did arts. They were ready to get married when they moved back here. Then Vivian employed Tony to do some work for her. I think it was maintenance stuff. One thing led to another, he became her personal assistant and then they got married.'

'He fell in love with Vivian?'

'Or her money. It's hard to say. Tony came from a poor family. Maybe he got dazzled by Vivian's wealth. I feel sorry for Melissa, though. She was pretty broken up by the whole thing.'

I nodded, thinking about the house in Berrajig. Vivian had made a fortune over the years. Tony could have been infatuated with her or her money. It was hard to tell. Kim and I thanked Shona and headed to the street. We were about to climb into my jeep when I noticed a familiar figure approaching.

'Hey Todd,' I said, and then my gaze slid to the woman at his side.

The burly police sergeant was wearing casual gear: jeans and a shirt that only served to emphasise his muscular physique. He smiled, but I could tell he was uneasy. 'Rosie,' he said. 'Kim. Nice to see you.' He noticed my focus on the strange woman. She was a brunette with short hair, stick skinny, and wearing a shift dress covered in tiny flowers. 'This is Yvonne, an old school friend of mine.'

She stuck out her hand. 'You must be the famous Rosie Ryan,' she said.

Kim added, 'And the not-so-famous Kim Chen.'

'Yvonne's staying for a while,' Todd explained.

'That must be nice for you,' I said and immediately thought the comment sounded narky. I turned to her. 'Enjoying Cape Carson?'

'I've only been here a couple of days,' Yvonne said. 'But it's lovely.'

Despite wanting to say a thousand things, none would come together into a coherent sentence. Maybe it was simply my own insecurities. Or perhaps it was how close Yvonne and Todd were to each other. An *intimate* distance.

After glancing at my watch, I told them I had to get moving, so I delivered a quick cheerio before getting into my car.

'Wow,' Kim said once she'd settled beside me, and the pair had wandered off. 'She's gorgeous.'

'Really? I didn't notice.'

My phone buzzed as a text message arrived. My discomfort at seeing the woman was replaced by a flush of excitement as I read my phone. 'Good news,' I said. 'Tony Hall's checked with the other attendees. We're going to a séance.'

4

Well, I thought. *Here we are.*

Tony Hall had met us at the front door. After taking us to our room in the west wing, where we'd stashed our bags, he'd led us back to the living room. Here, everyone was standing around, nursing what appeared to be non-alcoholic drinks. It was late in the day, the rain had finally cleared, and the afternoon sun was casting long shadows across the lake and lawn.

Tony leaned close. 'Probably a good idea if I introduce you around,' he said. 'First impressions count.'

There would be time after the séance, and in the morning, when I could properly interview people. Breaking the ice now would be a good start.

Tony led us to a couple standing uncomfortably in a corner. They were Alicia and Russell Warren, a sixtyish pair with greying hair and lined faces. The man looked grim as if he'd swallowed a slug, whereas Alicia wore a slightly dismayed expression. The look someone would wear if they stepped off a bus at the wrong stop.

'So you're the reporters,' Russell said briskly. He leaned heavily on a walking stick with a silver handle. 'We don't want our names used in your article. Or our pictures.'

'That's no problem,' I quickly assured them. 'More than anything, we want to know what brings people to seances. What you hope to get out of the experience.'

Pursing his lips, Russell looked ready to not say another word, but Alicia spoke up. 'It's my father,' she said. 'He was my friend. My dearest friend. But he died months ago. Six months now. Quite unexpectedly.'

'I'm sorry to hear that,' I said.

'Was he very old?' Kim inquired politely.

'Eighty-one,' Alicia answered. 'But in good health. *Excellent* health. His death could almost be considered *unusual*.'

Russell frowned. 'Alicia.'

'It *is* unusual,' she insisted, turning to him. 'They did something to him at that nursing home. Something wrong. And now they're covering it up.'

'We've requested an investigation into Gideon's death,' Russell said, sounding as if he were apologising for it.

Maybe it was more Alicia's idea than his as she continued. 'My father believed in the afterlife,' she said. 'He believed it was possible to speak to those who have passed. He can tell us if they hurt him. If they did anything wrong.'

'So that's what you're hoping to get from this?' I said. 'That seems fairly precise.'

I was familiar with the feedback that mediums gave people. It was so generic it could apply to anyone. Will I find true love? *Yes!* Should I change jobs? *Consider it!* Is it the right time for me to take a holiday? *Absolutely!*

I wondered how Vivian would handle specific queries like this. And then there were the dozens or hundreds of people who would live-stream the event.

All they would see was Vivian in the chapel. How did they get satisfaction from all this?

Thanking the pair, Tony steered us towards two women who were talking. Or, one was talking, anyway. The other looked like she couldn't get a word in.

'...several mediums have helped me speak to Gretchen,' she was saying. The woman was fiftyish, stout, and wore a white dress decorated in yellow and pink daisies. 'It's always so lovely catching up. It's like she's never gone.'

'Edwina Parkridge and Tania Knight.' Tony introduced us. 'Rosie and Kim are from the Gazette.'

'I don't want my photo taken,' Tania said quickly. She was skinny with short, brown hair starting to grey. 'Or my name mentioned.'

'That's perfectly fine,' I said. 'I can refer to you as a source.'

Edwina was more obliging. 'You can quote me,' she said. 'It's important that people know what's happening here.'

Kim spoke up. 'And that is...'

'Vivian and people like her see through the veil. They show us that death has no meaning.'

'You've been to mediums before?' I asked.

'Many times.' Edwina's chin wobbled. 'Ever since Gretchen passed over.'

'And Gretchen was...'

'My sister. A bowling ball accident.'

'She was killed by a bowling ball?'

'The police called it a freak accident, but there are no accidents. The man in the next bowling alley released the ball at the wrong time. Hit her in the head. Killed her instantly.' She leaned close. 'I was upset.'

'I suppose you would—'

'But I'm fine now. It's like Gretchen's taken a train to the next stop. I can talk to her any time.'

Kim hazarded. 'How long since she...er, took the train?'

'Ten years. It's like she never left.'

I wasn't sure I'd want to be conversing with family members ten years after they died. Some, I didn't want to talk to while they were alive!

'And you, Tania?' I said. 'May I ask what's brought you here?'

Tania ground her left foot into the floor. 'It's my son,' she said, not meeting my gaze. 'He drowned three years ago.'

'I'm sorry to hear that.'

Studying her face, I had the strangest feeling that I'd seen her before. Not anyone I had met or knew well.

Maybe I saw her on TV.

'What was your son's name?' I asked.

'Peter. He was twelve.'

Their reactions to losing their loved ones could not be more different. Whereas Edwina was exuberant, Tania was reserved. But there was something else too. Something evasive. Tania clearly didn't want to speak to us. Some people were like that. They saw the media as the enemy.

'So you're hoping to contact him,' I prompted.

'That's the idea.'

Kim spoke up. 'What do you think he'll say?'

Tania met our gaze. 'I don't know,' she said, her face unreadable. 'That's up to him.'

It was an odd remark. Almost flippant. *Maybe she's not a believer.* That would explain her apparent indifference to the whole thing. Maybe she was so desperate to speak to her dear son that she was trying this as a last resort.

There were more questions I wanted to ask, but this wasn't the time as Tony was already whisking us off to the remaining visitor. The elderly man stood at the window, standing still as a statue as he peered sightlessly out at the darkening lake.

Tony introduced the man as Sidney Langston. 'This is Rosie Ryan, the journalist,' Tony said. 'And Kim Chen, the photographer from the Gazette.'

Sidney didn't speak for a moment. He regarded us as if he were glancing at a piece of furniture. 'Nice to meet you both,' he said, finally. 'You've come to hear what our loved ones have to say?'

I wouldn't have quite put it like that. 'And to know what brings you to a séance,' I said. 'You've lost a loved one?'

'My wife. A car accident last year.' He gave a tight smile. 'Jill had just come to one of Vivian's sessions. She wanted to contact our daughter, who'd died. After the séance, Jill was driving home when the accident happened. Drove into a tree.'

'I'm sorry. That must have been terrible. You were married a long time?'

'Forty years.'

Tony inclined his head. 'I'll leave you to speak.'

After he disappeared down a hall, Sidney drew close to us. 'You're from the Gazette?'

I nodded.

'I don't have a high opinion of newspapers,' he said, pursing his lips. 'Try not to make this too sensational. People have lost loved ones. They don't want to be ridiculed. Everyone here has experienced enough pain.'

'I'll be mindful of people's feelings,' I assured him.

Sidney seemed about to say something more, but then he glanced over my shoulder, and a sudden hush fell over the room. Tony had reappeared, this time with Vivian at his side. She was wearing black again, but now her hair was in a bun. She wore no makeup, or if she did, it was so delicately applied as to be almost invisible. The rings on her fingers were embellished with blue, green, and orange gems. Her necklace was less gaudy than last time: silver with red and blue stones.

Vivian gazed across the room. 'Friends,' she said. 'Welcome to the Lake House. I know you've spoken to Tony, but most of you, I haven't met before.'

'Vivian,' Tony said. 'We're still waiting on someone. Kira McDonald. She hasn't turned up yet.'

'I've left the front gates open. We'll hear her if she rings at the door.' Vivian turned back to the group. 'We always begin these sessions with a tour of the property.'

Drinks were put down, and we trailed after Vivian toward the Scarlet room.

Considering the size of the house, the corridor was surprisingly squashed with everyone shoulder to shoulder.

'You're already familiar with the West wing,' Vivian said. 'Those are your guest quarters. This East end of the building is used for private meditation and prayer. The doors are lockable, so you're most welcome to use them as required.' We reached the Scarlet room and everyone filed inside. I gazed out at the chapel on the other side of the lake.

The gloom was so palpable that the tiny building already lay swamped in shadows. Recessed lights set into the ground lit the footpath around the lake.

Vivian explained the history of the chapel.

'So we'll be in here?' Alicia asked.

Vivian nodded. She pointed to the chapel. 'Your thoughts—and those who are streaming into the session—will be directed to me in the chapel. The chapel magnifies my connection with the spirit world.'

Kim leaned close. 'Can't she just ring up?'

I whispered. 'I don't think it works that way.'

Vivian led us back down the hallway to the end of the East wing. We passed an empty kitchen. I remembered Tony and Vivian saying cooking wasn't their forte. It looked like the chef was already gone.

We headed outside and followed the trail around the lake to the chapel. People squeezed in through the doorway one at a time while Vivian explained its history. Kim nudged me and gave a tiny nod to Sidney. He had an odd expression on his face. Something unreadable. A mixture of grief and anger. It was only there for a moment. Then he noticed us watching and forced a smile.

I wonder what's going through his head.

Edwina gave an excited giggle. 'I can feel something in the air,' she said. 'I'm no medium, but I can always sense when a place has a special energy.'

'The spirits use this place as a doorway to the other world,' Vivian said. 'The veil is thin between life and death. It's only natural that we should feel their presence.'

We continued around the lake back to the west end of the house. A half-drawn curtain revealed a bedroom illuminated only by a single lamp. I hadn't noticed it before, but this whole section of the building was Vivian and Tony's enormous bedroom. Through the curtain, I spotted a huge bed, an ensuite, and walk-in wardrobe.

That bedroom's bigger than most houses, I thought.

Handcrafted garden ornaments lined the ledge along the bottom of the vast plate glass window.

Edwina pointed. 'I love your ornaments,' she said. 'Did you make them?'

'They're by a local artist,' Vivian said. 'Bryan Trusk. Do you know him?'

'No, I don't.'

'He's terrific. I like to support local creatives.'

I looked more closely at them.

It's nice supporting local talent, I thought. *But they're not to my taste.*

One of them, a ceramic fish, had big ears. It reminded me of an old math's teacher I'd once had.

What was his name? Mister Helpman. That's right. He was always less than helpful.

Maths had never been my best subject.

We followed Vivian and Tony into the building and were soon traipsing back down the curving corridor to the living room. Here, Edwina asked if it would be all right to have a photo taken with Vivian.

'That would be fine,' Vivian said. 'Rosie? Can you take a picture?'

'Of course,' I said.

I snapped a photo of the women together, promising I'd send it to them later. A small knock came from the front door.

'That must be Kira McDonald,' Tony said.

He disappeared through to the foyer. I heard the door open and then Tony's surprised cry. 'What are you doing here?' he asked.

Peeping into the foyer, I saw a doe-eyed woman with a short, blonde bob. Skinny and pale, she wore a halter dress with a blue scarf.

'I had to come,' she was saying.

'It's over between us,' Tony hissed. 'You know that!'

I remembered back to what Kim had said about Tony's ex-fiancée. *This must be the jilted Melissa Martin.* Although she was attractive, her face was wrought with despair.

'But I need to see you.'

'Not now. We're holding a session tonight.'

'I know,' she said, her jaw clenching defiantly. 'I've booked for it.'

'What?'

'Under the name Kira McDonald.' She folded her arms. 'And what makes you think I'm here to see you? My mother died recently, and I need Vivian's help. I need to make contact.'

'I heard about your mother,' Tony said. 'And I'm sorry, but you can't be here.'

Vivian sailed past me into the foyer. 'Melissa,' she said. 'Did I hear correctly? Your mother has passed?'

Melissa's bottom lip quivered. 'Yes,' she said. 'Three weeks ago. Vivian, we may have had our differences—'

'That doesn't matter now,' Vivian said, dismissing the past with a wave of her hand. 'If you're here to *truly* connect with your mother, then you're welcome. You *are* here to connect with her?'

Melissa's eyes angled to the floor. 'My mother has had cancer for the last few years. She worsened recently, and I wasn't there when she passed. I'd been at the hospital with her all night. I didn't want to leave her alone. I went out to get a glass of water. When I returned...' Melissa wiped away an angry tear. 'I should have been there. Right at the end. I *should* have been there.'

Tony turned to his wife. 'Vivian,' he said. 'Are you sure—'

Vivian continued. 'Melissa,' she said. 'You won't upset our other guests? You understand they have their own wounds to heal.'

Melissa might have been more satisfied if Vivian had thrown her out. This unexpected gesture of generosity had caught her unawares. 'I understand,' she said, quietly. She looked like a small girl, an insecure child. 'There'll be no trouble.'

Tony's gaze switched from Vivian to Melissa. As to what he was thinking, I could only guess. He'd been through a breakup with Melissa, and maybe he felt that part of his life was over and he could move on. There was relief in that. I'd been through a similar journey. Leaving emotional upheaval behind allowed you to move forward.

But now it wasn't over. Not now.

This is terrible, I thought. *I'd want her out of the house—no matter what.*

Vivian turned to Tony. 'Darling,' she said. 'Are you all right with this?'

Her husband looked like he was caught between a rock and a hard place. He regarded the two women silently before turning to Vivian. 'I'm fine,' he told her. 'As long as this evening's proceedings aren't disrupted.'

Melissa swallowed. 'I won't cause any trouble,' she said. 'I promise.'

5

'This isn't bad,' Kim said. 'Not like mum used to make, but not bad.'

After the meeting in the living room, and then Melissa's dramatic appearance, everyone had retired to their chambers to have dinner and prepare for the evening ahead.

Our bedroom looked out onto the lake and the bush beyond. Darkness had settled; the only illumination was the tiny lights around the lake and a final dusty glow that creased the horizon.

Our room was like a finely styled hotel room; the furniture was coloured mahogany, the curtains were white and heavy, and the bathroom was clad in dark stone. Water gurgled through a water feature on a side table.

There was no television. Maybe that was to keep everyone focused.

Tony had brought dinner on a trolley. Kim had ordered a shepherd's pie while I'd chosen a pizza. It was tasty, although vaguely reminiscent of airline food.

There was something slightly odd in seeing the handsome and well-dressed Tony pushing a food trolley about. I got the impression he did most of the work around here. Although they had servants, I guessed that Tony and Vivian kept their business to themselves.

'You're right,' I said, swallowing a mouthful of pizza. 'This is okay.'

'A man who can cook is a good thing to have around the house,' she said, raising an eyebrow. 'I wonder what Todd's cooking is like.'

One of Kim's ongoing projects was finding a new partner for me.

'Kim,' I said. 'Nothing is happening with Todd.'

'I know! That's the problem!'

'Love will come along when it's ready.'

'Now you sound like a character in a Hallmark movie. Todd's available. You need to track him down and drag him back to your lair.'

'I'm not a sabre-toothed tiger.'

'Then you need to be.' She put down her fork. 'Rosie, what's happening with that big hunky police sergeant?'

I sat back and peered out at the night. 'I'm not sure,' I said. 'We seem to be on again and off again—and we were never on in the first place.'

'And Yvonne?'

My mind returned to Todd's friend. What had he said? *This is Yvonne, an old school friend.* That meant they had history. Maybe a lot of it. They may have been more than friends. Could have even dated.

That was none of my business. Todd was a free agent. He could date anyone he wanted. Although…

Kim had picked up her fork and swallowed the last of her pie. 'You are literally turning green.'

'Huh?'

'Jealousy,' she said. 'You look like you want to punch Yvonne in the nose.'

'Don't be ridiculous,' I spluttered. 'I don't go punching random people who I don't know.'

'It *is* better if you know them first.'

I ignored her and got back to the issue of Todd and me. 'It's our jobs,' I said. 'I'm a journalist, and he's a cop. It's my job to discover information, and it's his to keep it to himself. That's like oil and water. The two don't mix.'

'But you have been out on a few dates.'

'I'm not sure I'd call them dates. And what are we supposed to talk about? We can't talk about our jobs because that information is classified.'

'Rosie,' Kim said. 'There's more to life than work.'

I was about to point out to Kim that I was well aware of this when I heard sniffling from the hall.

Kim leaned close. 'Is that someone crying?'

'I think so.'

I stuck my head out. Most doors were closed, but the one next to ours was half-open. Kim and I crept down to it.

'Melissa?' I said.

The woman looked up despondently from her meal tray, her face red and streaked with tears. 'Oh,' she said. 'Hi. Sorry about that.'

'Is it Tony?' Kim asked.

I shot a look at Kim. She could be terribly direct at times. But it was one way to discover what was wrong.

Melissa impatiently wiped away her tears. 'Sorry,' she said. 'I didn't know it would be this tough.'

I remembered the first few times I'd seen my ex-husband George wandering around the streets of Cape Carson with his new girlfriend. It was like being hit with a sledgehammer. 'Breakups are hard,' I said sympathetically. 'It takes time to work your way through things.'

'Can we come in?' Kim asked.

Melissa nodded, and we sat down with her.

'It's been difficult,' Melissa said, playing with her scarf. 'Dad has early-onset dementia, and Tony broke it off with me. Now with Mum dying...'

She looked ready to burst into tears again.

'So you're hoping to contact your mother?' I said, trying not to sound sceptical. 'Is that really what brought you here?'

'Mum and I were really close,' Melissa said. 'She was my best friend. Lifted me up when I was down. When Tony walked out, Mum was there to support me.'

'So you believe Vivian can help you?'

'There are stories all over the internet about Vivian putting people in contact with loved ones. And Vivian is kind. *Terribly* kind. It would be easier if she were awful!' She stopped. 'And Tony believes in her. If he believes, then I believe. Despite what's happened, I know that he's ethical. He's *always* been like that.'

'Do you still have feelings for him?' Kim asked.

Melissa hesitated. 'I accept that he doesn't love me anymore,' she said. 'But you can't just turn off your feelings like a switch. If he walked out on Vivian today, I'm not sure what I'd do.'

'And he loves Vivian?' I said. 'You don't think her money...'

Melissa gave a bitter laugh. 'I wish it were her money,' she said. 'No. It was love at first sight. We met her at a book launch. You see how handsome Tony is. Women have always fallen for him. The problem is, this time, it was a two-way street. Their eyes met, and it was like no one else existed. He did some IT work for her. Then he became her personal assistant. I knew it was over then.' She wiped away an angry tear. 'I'm sorry. This is hard.'

A single gong sounded in the living room. That was a ten-minute warning. Two gongs would mean it was time to assemble in the Scarlet room.

Leaving Kim with Melissa, I collected all our tableware and went to the living room, where the empty cart waited. I was about to leave when Tony emerged from the West wing hallway.

'Oh, hello Rosie,' he said. 'How are you finding it all?'

'Fine. The people are an interesting mix.'

'Including Melissa?'

I raised an eyebrow.

'Sorry,' Tony apologised. 'I heard you speaking in her room. Seeing her was quite a surprise.'

'She wants to contact her mother.'

'I can understand that.' He peered outside at the black lake. 'I knew her mother, Jenny. She hadn't been well for a long time, and I can understand Melissa wanting to make contact. It might change her life if Vivian can establish communication. Give Melissa some peace.'

It was hard to know what to say. 'I suppose Vivian gives people closure,' I said.

Tony smiled humourlessly. 'Spoken like a true unbeliever.' He held up a hand. 'I understand. I really do. I was the same. I was hired to look after her IT systems. Then she let me attend one of her sessions.' He shook his head. 'Vivian told me things she couldn't possibly know. Things about my grandfather. I lost him when I was young. Only eleven. He and I used to go on foraging walks through the bush. And Vivian told me things that I'd never told anyone. She told me things that only he and I would know.' Tony's eyes fixed on me. 'Believe me—Vivian's the real deal.'

6

'No matter what happens tonight,' Vivian said, 'I will ask that you follow Tony's every command. We are dealing with powerful forces, and the curtain separating this world from the next is fragile. If one of you breaks the circle, you will break it for everyone.'

Vivian was standing in the doorway of the Scarlet room. The rest of us were seated around the table. From where I was sitting, I had a clear view of the lake and the bush. The tiny chapel lay nestled in darkness. The little lights set into the footpath trailed around the path's edge, creating tiny pools of illumination.

Kim sat to my left, with Alicia to my right. Beyond her were Russell, Edwina, Tania, Melissa, Sidney, and Tony. My eyes angled up to the television screen behind Tony. It read:

Live-streaming: active

Participants: 256

Goodness, I thought. That's people from all over the world.

And we haven't even started yet.

The opposite screen still lay in darkness.

'No one should speak directly to Vivian while she's in contact with the spirit world,' Tony said. 'It can cause irreparable harm to her psychic soul that can take days, even weeks, to heal.'

'Vivian,' Alicia said. 'I need to speak to my father. I need to know if he was harmed at that horrible place!'

'The spirits come to me as they see fit,' Vivian explained. 'They are not ours to order, just as they cannot control our actions. If they wish to communicate, they will.'

'Gretchen will contact me,' Edwina beamed. 'She always does. Gretchen has *always* been a chatterbox.'

Drrrrrriinnnggg!

The ring of the phone stopped the conversation.

Melissa sheepishly took out her mobile phone and glanced at the screen. 'I'm so sorry,' she said. 'I must take this. It's my father. He's been unwell.'

'Of course,' Vivian said.

Melissa hurried out to the living room.

'Tony,' Vivian said. 'The live streaming link is active to the chapel?'

He peered down at the control panel set into the table. 'It is.'

'Will we wait for Melissa?' Vivian asked.

'I'm sure she won't be long.'

'Then I'll leave you,' she continued. 'Remember, you must follow Tony's instructions to the letter.' She cast her gaze across the table as she issued one final warning. '*I must stay completely focused.*'

Upon saying this, Vivian nodded and turned left out the door. No one spoke. Kim looked apprehensive. Tony was stony-faced. Alicia looked close to tears. Russell took her hand and gave it a reassuring squeeze. Edwina, by comparison, could hardly contain her excitement.

She reminded me of one of those women at bingo who is on the verge of having the winning number announced.

Tania's bottom lip was trembling. I thought about what she'd said about her son. *He drowned three years ago.* What a terrible thing to experience. It was hard to read her expression. I wasn't sure if she was angry or upset. Maybe both. That kind of tragedy could affect someone in a myriad of ways.

Finally, my eyes rested on Sidney Langston. His face was unreadable—but not his hands. They were clenched tightly together, the knuckles white. He was staring into space, and for a second, I saw his reserve break. His eyes grew watery, and I remembered what he'd said about his wife.

After the séance, Jill was driving home when the accident happened. Drove into a tree.

It must have been a terrible shock for him. For all these

people. What brought them together was the desire to communicate with their loved ones. To set their minds at ease.

My eyes angled up to the live-streaming monitor.

The number on it had increased. It now read:

Live-streaming: active

Participants: 479

Regret churned in my gut. An article about Vivian would only serve as advertising. Still, this was news. It wasn't my job to expose her. Only to tell people what was happening.

The television screen opposite Tony flickered to life. At the same instant, I saw a small rectangle of light appear in the dark bushes as Vivian entered the chapel. Then the door closed behind her and the bush darkened again.

My attention returned to the screen. Vivian rounded the small table in the centre of the chapel and sat.

'This is so exciting!' Edwina declared. 'I do hope—'

'Silence!' Tony said sharply.

The words froze on Edwina's lips.

Vivian peered up at the camera. 'Tony.' Her voice came over the loud speakers. 'Can you hear me?'

'I can,' he answered.

Vivian continued. 'I welcome you all to this session,' she said. 'To those in the Scarlet room, I remind you to stay seated at all times during the séance. Once made, it's dangerous to break the connection.'

'I hope I don't need a bathroom break,' Kim muttered.

Tony shot her a look. If Vivian heard, she gave no indication as she continued.

'To those who are live-streaming into this event, I wish you well. There are visitors from the spirit realm who wish to connect; this is their only chance. If someone makes contact, I urge you to remain calm. Your connections are purposefully muted so everyone can stay connected.'

I had to hand it to Vivian. She was a true master of ceremonies. I wasn't sure if she believed the hogs wallop she was espousing or if it was a complete con. Either way, she was believable.

'I will begin with a prayer,' Vivian said. '*From ancient dawns to the end of time, we are joined here to...*'

Her voice droned on. I wondered how many times Vivian had recited the same prayer. Despite its length, she seemed to have it memorised.

'*...make contact with those who have passed...*'

I wondered where Melissa had gone. The séance proper would begin soon and she wanted to be here for it.

'*...from now till forever, we are all joined as one to...*'

There was movement from behind me as Melissa crept into the room. Giving us an apologetic look, she put her phone away and sat down between Tania and Sidney.

A flash of annoyance crossed Tony's face as he stared at her, and Melissa self-consciously rubbed her bare throat.

Sorry, she mouthed.

Tony turned away.

Vivian's prayer finally came to an end. 'Tony,' she said. 'Please ask the attendees to join hands.'

'Of course,' Tony replied. 'Everyone, please take the hand of the person beside you.'

We did as instructed. Kim's hand on mine was light, whereas Alicia gripped my hand like a vice. Her face was a mixture of dread and hope.

You poor woman, I thought. *I hope you get what you need from this.*

Returning my gaze to the screen, I watched Vivian lay her hands flat on the table as she closed her eyes and began breathing deeply. Her head dropped.

I thought about my grandfather, Frank Ryan. For the first time, I wondered what it would be like to speak to him again. My throat grew thick with emotion. He and Nan had been married for sixty years, and he had been one of my best friends. It would be wonderful to have one final conversation with him. To know that he was all right...

'I can see the curtain.' Vivian's voice was so low it was almost guttural. 'People are on the other side. It's hard to make them out. There's a woman. A man. Another woman. A child.'

The atmosphere in the room was palpable. My nerves were

jangling—and I didn't know why.

This is ridiculous! It's impossible to contact the dead!

But if it were possible...

Everyone's gaze was fixed on the monitor. Vivian's eyes were still closed, and she was breathing hard. She lifted her head sharply.

'There's a child here,' she said. 'A little boy.'

Tania gasped. 'My son,' she said. 'Please...Peter...'

'It's me, mum.' The voice coming from Vivian was high-pitched, like a young boy. 'It's Peter.'

Tania's resolve broke, and she wept.

'I'm all right, mum,' the voice emanating from Vivian said. 'I'm okay. I was swimming in the water, and then I fell asleep. When I awoke, I was here. I'm safe, and there's love everywhere.'

'Peter...Peter...' Tania said, a tear running down her cheek. 'Is grandma there?'

'Goodbye mum,' the voice said. 'Goodbye.'

'Peter,' Tania pleaded. 'Please tell me more.'

'Someone else is coming through the curtain,' Vivian said in her own voice. 'There are several people here. It's a woman. She's bright and happy. Full of life—'

'It's Gretchen!' Edwina cried. 'It must be her!'

'Edwina?' Vivian smiled as if making a joke. 'It's me! Gretchen!'

'Gretchen! It's so good to hear your voice! Are you—'

'I've never had so much fun! There is so much kindness and love here. It's a place of love. It's wonderful here. And I don't blame anyone for the accident. It's just one of those things. There was a moment of pain, and then I awoke here—'

'Is Uncle Stanley there?' Edwina asked. 'I'd love—'

'*Shhh*,' Tony said in a low voice. 'We don't command the spirits. They come and go as they wish.'

Suitably chastised, Edwina nodded and pursed her lips.

Vivian had ignored the exchange entirely and continued to speak. '...someone else is coming through,' she said. 'It's a man. An elderly man. He wants to speak to Alicia.' Her voice dropped down low. 'Alicia, my darling. I'm all right. Know that. My time had come. My body had endured enough.'

Alicia was gripping my hand so hard it was hurting. I would have let go, except I doubted I could. Tears poured down the woman's face.

'Dad!' she said. 'The nursing home...did they...'

'I'm at peace,' Vivian continued in the same deep voice. 'I'm here with my brothers William and Terry. All is fine. No one is to blame for what happened. Everything has its time, and my time is here and now.' Vivian's voice resumed her usual tone. 'There's a woman here. A kind woman. Someone I knew but was taken suddenly.'

My eyes shot to Sidney as he leaned forward. He opened his

mouth as if to speak but clamped his lips together.

'My darling Sidney,' Vivian said, her voice now that of an older woman. 'I am in a kind place. I'm here with your mother and father. All is well. And Mia is here. She asks that you release the pain in your heart. There is freedom in release.'

Sidney Langston slowly nodded as Vivian's head dropped again. The next time she looked up, she stared into the camera. 'There are many, many people on the other side, visitors with messages for those at home,' she said. 'They want their thoughts known. I'm picking up a woman who was a father to Rachel. He regrets some things he said and wants her to move on with her life—'

My eyes moved around the table and settled on Edwina.

There was something about her face. She'd been smiling before. Now her expression seemed stuck. Frozen. It was like someone who had bitten into an apple and found a worm.

What's going through her mind?

Vivian's voice continued.

'...a man named John wants to send his love to Sam,' she intoned. 'He says that all is well...'

Kim glanced at me, raising an eyebrow. Alicia's grip on my hand had loosened. A small smile played on her lips. Even Russell looked more relaxed. Melissa's eye met mine, and she gave an almost imperceptible shrug. No message had come through from her mother, but she seemed resigned to it.

How strange, I thought. *If Vivian's a fraud, why didn't she make up something to keep Melissa satisfied? It made no sense. Unless Vivian wanted to hurt her?*

No. There was another, even weirder possibility, that Vivian really was a medium, and Melissa's mother had not been ready to make contact.

'...Jason is sorry,' Vivian was saying. 'He regrets the nasty things he said. Words were spoken in anger and didn't reflect what was in his heart...'

The list of names continued for the next few minutes before finally ending when Vivian eventually fell silent. She let out a long breath, and bowed her head before wearily gazing up at the camera. 'Many spirits on the other side wanted to make contact,' she said. 'I am exhausted.'

'We've been fortunate,' Tony said. 'I thank everyone who live-streamed in tonight. I'm glad that Vivian was able to make contact with some of your loved ones. A recording of the event will be available later in the week. Thank you for your attendance.'

I glanced up at the monitor. The final number on it was *781*.

The screen went black as the live-streaming disconnected.

'Vivian,' Tony said. 'We'll see you back in the living room.' He glanced first at Melissa and then at the rest of us. 'It's been an emotional evening.'

Vivian sat for a moment longer. Then she got up from her

seat, crossed to the door, and the chapel went dark. Everyone was still holding hands, so Tony told us to let go, give our hands a shake and relax. The tension in the room had vanished, almost as if a switch had been turned, but everyone was silent with their own thoughts.

'Tonight, there were many spirits on the other side,' Tony said. 'Sometimes it's like that. We'll return to the living room where we can unpack our thoughts.'

A few minutes later, we were back at the picture windows overlooking the darkened lake. Alicia and Russell chatted in low voices. Edwina was beaming and chattering incessantly to Sidney, who was nodding without comment. Melissa stood in the corner, alone with her own thoughts.

Tania, in the opposite corner, did the same.

Tony made his way around the room with the drinks cart, offering people refreshments. Reaching Tania, he stopped to whisper to her as she wiped a tear away.

Kim took me aside. 'Rosie,' she said, her voice low. 'What did you make of all that?'

'I don't know,' I confessed. 'Did you feel...'

'Uneasy? Afraid? As if the gates of Hell had been opened—'

'Let's just leave it at uneasy,' I interrupted. 'Vivian is *quite* a performer.'

Kim nodded. 'It was weird. I don't know if mediums are real or not, but Vivian was convincing.' She leaned closer. 'You don't think this could be legitimate?'

'No.' I shook my head resolutely. 'It's not possible.'

It couldn't be real. People couldn't contact the dead. The whole idea was ridiculous.

And yet—Vivian was *very* convincing.

Tony pushed the cart over. 'Ladies,' he said. 'How did you find that?'

'Interesting,' I said diplomatically. 'Vivian's not back yet?'

'No. She normally comes straight from the chapel. I wonder what's keeping her.'

I thought about her in that tiny room. A photo of Vivian in the chapel with all that old stonework behind her could be striking. It might even make the front page. If Vivian were still in the chapel, possibly Kim and I could take some photos.

'Would that be all right?' I asked.

'I'm sure that would be fine.'

He led us down the corridor, past the bedrooms, and out the west door of the house. The cool evening air closed in around us as we rounded the lake. Everything was in darkness apart from the tiny lights in the path.

Nearing the chapel, a tiny rectangle of light pushed out from under the door.

'Vivian could be meditating,' Tony said reflectively. 'She does that sometimes, although it's a cold night to be out here, and it gets even colder in the chapel.'

I inhaled.

'Do you smell that?' I asked.

Kim sniffed. 'It smells like a fire,' she said. 'Or some kind of chemical.'

I knew that smell, and I didn't like it. 'I think a gun's been fired,' I said.

'Uh...okay,' Kim said. 'And we're heading *towards* it?'

Tony's pace increased, and he shoved open the door. The room appeared empty as we crowded inside. Then Tony Hall let out a piteous cry followed by yelling of *no, no, no*. Circling around the table, we saw a tangle of bodies and blood. Lots of blood. Vivian Shelly lay on her back, half-buried under a man who wore a balaclava and a dark suit. A knife protruded from the man's chest, whereas Vivian Shelly had been shot at least once. Maybe twice. The gun lay beside them.

Tony Hall shrieked in torment as he shoved the killer's body aside and pulled Vivian to him. 'No!' he sobbed. 'You can't be gone. My darling, come back to me...'

7

'Well,' Todd Parker said. 'You've done it again.'

I glared at him. 'Done *what* again?' I demanded. 'My lawful duty in reporting that a murder—no, *two* murders have been committed?'

We were in the Scarlet Room at Vivian's place. After discovering the bodies, I'd rung the police before delivering the bad news to the attendees. Their first reaction had been flat-out disbelief. It was understandable. Vivian Shelly had been alive and well only minutes before. Then disbelief had transformed into shock and confusion as reality had set in. This was after Kim and I had virtually dragged Tony Hall back to the house. We had left him, sobbing and helpless, in his bedroom.

'Ringing us about a murder is what you're supposed to do,' Todd said firmly. 'But does it always have to be you?'

Kim held up a small hand. 'I'll do it next time.'

Todd rolled his eyes. 'I don't want *either of you* ringing us about murders. There are already *far* too many murders in

Cape Carson.' He struggled to speak. 'Ed from the Pastry shop never rings up.'

'There's still time,' I assured him. 'Anyway, this seems to be an open and shut case.'

'A robbery gone wrong,' Todd agreed, nodding. 'The intruder entered through the rear chapel door. Robbery appears to have been the motive. There was a struggle. Judging by the defensive wounds on Vivian's hands, he may have threatened her with the knife.'

'So how did that end up in him?' Kim asked.

'We'll have to look at it closer, but my guess is she somehow turned the tables. Struggled the knife away and stabbed him as he produced the gun. She's been shot twice by the look of it.'

'Can we take another look at the crime scene?' I asked. 'There's something I'd like to check.'

Todd frowned. 'We don't normally allow members of the public to examine our crime scenes,' he said. 'It's sort of a police thing.'

'It might help your investigation.'

Grudgingly, Todd agreed, and we filed down the corridor past the living room. It was like looking at a painting; everyone seemed frozen in place. Melissa was peering at the dark lake. Edwina thoughtfully nursed a glass of soda. Alicia and Russell huddled silently together, holding hands. Tania was on her phone, sending a message.

The only person who seemed out of place was Sidney. The man looked oddly satisfied, in fact, almost *jubilant* as he stood in the corner, a glass of water in hand. His eyes angled to mine as we passed, and he turned away.

Very odd.

We continued out the west end of the building and back to the chapel. Constable Jim Turner had turned up and was making notes as a police photographer took pictures. My eyes scanned the scene. The assailant's body had been pushed to one side, but Vivian Shelly still lay in the same position on her back. The scene was identical to how it had been when we'd rung the police—and that worried me.

'There's no bag,' I said.

'What?' Todd said.

'The thief didn't bring a bag with him,' I said. 'That can't be normal.'

'It's more normal than you'd think. Criminals aren't always the most logical people.'

'So the thief brought a knife and a gun with him,' I said. 'But no bag.'

Todd nodded to the man's body. The balaclava over his head had been pulled off to reveal a blonde-haired man. His handsome face had been marred by a teardrop tattoo under one eye. I thought he'd been wearing a suit before, but he was actually more casually dressed. He wore a jacket, t-shirt and jeans: all black, the perfect colour to stay hidden in the dark.

So why was there no bag?

'There are several pockets in that jacket,' Todd pointed out. 'They're more than enough if you're stealing jewellery. And he probably didn't intend to use the gun or the knife. Most of these guys use the threat of violence. Nothing more. It looks like things got out of hand.'

Kim spoke up. 'There's something else, too.'

Todd sighed. 'Which is?'

'We didn't hear gunshots.'

The policeman tapped on the stone wall. 'I'm guessing the door was shut? The walls are a foot thick, and the door's solid oak.' He pointed to the gun. 'And that's a twenty-two. They don't make a lot of noise.'

'But we should have heard something,' I insisted.

'You may not have noticed,' Todd said. 'From what you've said, the assault happened immediately after the séance ended. That means you were all either in the hallway or the living room. That's some distance from here. And you were busy talking. A twenty-two makes a sound like a loud pop.'

I suppose Todd was right. All our attention was on what had happened during the séance. The gun fired, and we didn't notice. Besides, whether we heard the gun or not was a moot point. Vivian had been shot twice, which obviously happened after the séance ended.

I peered down at the knife. It was a steak knife, as if from a set. There was nothing particularly distinctive about it. The necklace lay in a tangled pile, the green stones glittering in the light. My eyes shifted to Vivian's body and I remembered what she'd said.

'I can see the curtain...People are on the other side...'

Well, I thought. *Now she's on the other side too.*

There was movement in the doorway behind us, and Tony Hall appeared. The poor man looked like he'd aged twenty years.

'Tony,' Todd said. 'You need to wait in the living room with everyone else.'

He nodded. 'I will,' he said. 'But there's something I need to check first. I might know the man who killed her.' He hesitated. 'Will you let me take another look at him?'

The policeman reluctantly agreed. Tony squeezed into the room, and took a tiny regretful look at his wife before focusing on the man. 'No,' he said, finally. 'I've never seen him before.'

'You're sure?' Todd asked.

'I suppose he could have been one of Vivian's clients. That's possible. But I don't recognise him.'

Todd suggested they return to the Lake House. Tony Hall gave his wife a final soulful glance before we emerged from the tiny room and into the cold night air.

'Of course,' Tony continued, 'Vivian's jewellery wasn't

worth anything. It's just bling. She likes…liked to wear it. Made her feel dressed up.'

'I see,' Todd said thoughtfully. 'There's a track that leads in from a back road. We found a car there. Probably his.'

Tony nodded. 'The front of the property is well guarded,' he said. 'But there's nothing at the back. We use that track sometimes to go on walks. We do…did that sometimes.'

We entered the house. It had been a long day, and it wasn't ending soon. There were interviews to be done, and none of the guests could stay overnight.

Fortunately, Todd had gotten our statements so Kim and I could leave while the others remained. After grabbing our luggage, we headed out to my jeep as a van from the coroner's office arrived.

It was late, after midnight, and the air was freezing and the sky clear. I glanced up to see the vast sweep of the galaxy above us, like glowing sand on an ebony carpet. We climbed exhausted into my jeep, and I started the engine.

'My goodness,' I said. 'What a night.'

'You're telling me,' Kim said. 'I thought we'd be talking to dead people. Not seeing them in person.'

8

'Medium *Doesn't* Forsee Her Own Death,' Harry Blackshore chortled. 'What a headline!'

I was sitting opposite him in his office. It had been a busy morning. After working on several articles, including one on the murder of Vivian Shelly, I was finally filling Harry in on the night's events. 'Harry,' I admonished. 'She wasn't peering into a crystal ball. Vivian Shelly was speaking to the dead.'

'Must be easier than ever now. Doesn't have to go through all the mumbo-jumbo.'

'You're incorrigible.'

'At least you know the meaning of that word. Jay was trying to tell me yesterday that assent had something to do with mountain climbing.'

I sighed. 'It's easy to get ascent and assent mixed up,' I said. 'Although, I must agree that no one has ever climbed an agreement.'

'By the way, have you contacted Charlie yet?'

Oh gosh, I groaned. *Charlie and his totems.*

'Not yet. I'll get to it. I promise.'

I returned to my office and slumped down at my desk, where I found Jay glaring at me reproachfully.

'Harry told you about the mountain climbing, didn't he?' Jay said.

'I'm afraid so.'

'I'll never live that one down.'

'Probably not.' I glanced at my watch. It was almost lunchtime, and I'd only had one coffee. I decided that I needed another, or I might not survive the day. Taking Trixie with me, I headed down to Sandy's. I had almost reached the diner when Wanda Gibson came barrelling around the corner. She was taking her cat, Bastet, on one of her regular walks.

Trixie whined. Although she was a good dog in many ways, she always found it hard to deal with Wanda's walnut-coloured Abyssinian. Perhaps she found it unnatural that a cat could trot down the road on a leash in the same fashion as a dog.

'Rosie Ryan!' Wanda boomed. 'I heard about the death of that woman! The medium!'

I said she'd been murdered and explained the circumstances.

'Is that what really happened?' Wanda queried. 'You recall from our book club reading, how often the husband murders the wife? Or the wife murders the husband?'

'All wives want to murder their husbands sometimes,' I

quipped. 'There should probably be a clause in the marriage contract allowing it. But in this case, it was a simple burglary gone wrong. An open and shut case.'

Wanda rolled her eyes. 'They often seem that way,' she said. 'You recall *The Murder of Emily Horsham*? The wife was thought to have drowned at the beach? Then the detective recalled that she suffered from aquaphobia—a fear of water. She would never have gone swimming.'

I thought about the tangle of bodies: Vivian and the man locked in a death embrace. 'I'll keep it in mind,' I assured her, but not too seriously.

Continuing on, I was at the front step of the diner as someone else arrived at the same moment.

'Sadie!' I said.

'Hello Rosie,' Sadie replied. She was a slim forty-year-old woman with auburn hair and brown eyes. Today, she wore skin-tight blue jeans, t-shirt, and a bomber jacket, and had brought along her poodle, Lady Cha-Cha. Trixie and Lady Cha-Cha gave each other a good sniffing as Sadie continued. 'Haven't seen you around lately.'

Although my daughter Amanda had been in contact with George, I'd made a point of keeping out of his way. 'I've been busy,' I fibbed. 'Are you getting coffee?'

'Tea.'

We headed inside, ordered drinks, and discussed everything except what had happened with Nico. Sadie was a lovely lady—a vast improvement on George's previous girl-friend—and it was a shame our relationship was strained.

Saying goodbye to her, I returned to work, where Harry had gone through my stories. He called me into his office.

'You've missed something here,' he said. 'It sounds like that front gate was pretty imposing.'

'They obviously didn't want visitors.'

'Were they afraid? Had they been threatened?'

I remembered what Tony had said about receiving nasty parcels. 'Tony Hall mentioned some unpleasant messages,' I said. 'It could be worthwhile knowing what they contained.'

I said I'd ring and ask. A few minutes later, I had Tony Hall on the phone. I began by querying how he was coping with Vivian's loss.

'It's stressful,' Tony said thickly. 'Vivian always said it was harder for those left behind. For those who have passed, it's like walking through a door. One moment we're here, the next we're on the other side. It's our loved ones who must deal with the aftermath.'

'Whenever someone dies—even when it's expected—it's a terrible shock.' The death of my grandfather had been awful. He'd fallen asleep on the couch one day and not awoken. 'I did have a question that I was hoping you could answer. That's an impressive gate on the front entrance. Did you and Vivian feel you needed protection?'

Tony hesitated. 'We've always received strange letters from people,' he said. 'Threatening messages from people who don't appreciate what we do. Of late, though, we've had a lot of nasty mail. A dead rat, even.'

'Did you contact the police?'

'There didn't seem any reason. Like I say, we often got threatening mail.'

'You didn't mention this to the police last night?'

'Vivian's death didn't seem related.'

I asked if I could take a look at the letters. Although Tony sounded less than enthusiastic, he reluctantly agreed. An hour later, I was pulling up outside the Lake House and climbing out of my jeep.

A solitary crow sat on a branch and cawed mournfully at me. It seemed oddly appropriate considering there'd just been a death. I left Trixie in the car with the window down. She whined.

'Don't be like that,' I said. 'This isn't a dog-friendly house.'

I made my way to the front door and knocked.

Tony answered a moment later, looking unshaven and his hair dishevelled. He looked a far cry from the confident man I'd first met.

'Sorry to intrude,' I said. 'I'm sure you must have a lot happening.'

He shrugged. 'The dead don't arrange funerals,' he said. 'That's the job of the living.'

Tony invited me inside, and a few minutes later, I was in his office with half a dozen letters before me. They were a sobering read.

'*You people are evil and should die,*' I read one aloud and then the next. '*Fraudsters like you should be hung, drawn, and quartered.*'

'Definitely not a fan,' Tony said, smiling sadly. 'As I said, there was also the rat, but it's long gone. The dungeon note mentions rats.'

I scanned the message: *You should be thrown into a dungeon and eaten by rats.*

Each letter had been typed in large, black capitals, Times New Roman, by the look of it, and folded twice to fit into the envelopes.

Fortunately, Tony had kept these. They'd been posted from Cape Carson. The address on the front had been printed onto a sticky label.

The letters had arrived a few months apart over the last year.

'This is the latest one?' I said, examining the notes. 'It came about three months ago? So the gap's been longer this time.'

'The sender may have gotten sick of us and started targeting someone else.'

I asked if I could take them with me, and Tony agreed, saying they were useless to him anyway. He put them into a clear, plastic envelope and gave them to me. Wishing Tony all the best, I said goodbye and returned to my car, where Trixie was waiting.

She gave a single happy bark.

'Good girl,' I said and gave her a doggy snack. 'You are so patient.'

Trixie panted happily.

It was late in the day, and the sky was darkening. Reaching Cape Carson, I realised I had a message on my phone, so I pulled over to read it.

'Oh, bother!' I groaned.

Don't forget our painting class! Olga awaits!

The last thing I felt like doing was attending a painting class. Surely there was already enough bad art without me adding to it? Did the world really need another awful painting?

Anyway, I'd agreed to attend, so there was no getting out of it.

Half an hour later, I was pulling up outside the Community Centre on First Avenue. The place was an old weatherboard building down the street from the library and council. The classes here included yoga, martial arts, flower arranging, and cooking. I'd even been here learning Spanish, but I gave up when I kept confusing my male and female pronouns and accidentally called the teacher a cabbage.

I stumbled into the room to find half a dozen easels facing a selection of fruit. Kim had saved an easel for me. She waved me over.

'I was worried you wouldn't get here in time,' she said.

'Me too. If I'd left it for another hour, I wouldn't need to come at all.'

'Don't be like that. This class is supposed to release your hidden artistic talent.'

'That won't be easy. My artistic talent is *very* hidden.'

Olga Farago, aka The Spider, came bustling into the room. She was a big middle-aged woman with wild greying hair that had never seen a brush and long fingernails with emerald polish. She wore an oversized shirt, a shawl, baggy pants, and high-heeled shoes.

She looked nothing like a spider or an insect of any kind. Actually, she looked like a homeless person seeking a shelter.

'Good grief,' I whispered to Kim. 'She looks a bit rough.'

'Don't be silly!' Kim scolded me. 'She's a respected artist! Shortlisted for the Archibald Prize!'

Maybe, I thought. *But she didn't win it.*

As Olga plonked her bag onto the teacher's desk, I glanced about the room at the other attendees. A few faces I recognised from around the town. Father Tyler from Saint Michael's Church had attended; he wore casual clothing. There was Betty Sawyer, a chubby, bespeckled woman with greying hair whom I'd written about some months before. Beside her was Samantha Greco from the town bakery and Ellie Applegate from my office. A few others I knew by sight but not by name.

Olga strode to the middle of the room, planting hands on hips. 'Welcome!' she announced in an accent that sounded vaguely Hungarian. 'You have signed up for my art class, and I want to know why.' She pointed to Father Tyler. 'You! Why are you here?'

The priest withered under her glare. 'Uh,' he said. 'Well, I thought it would be nice to paint some religious iconography. Maybe a portrait or two—'

'*Wrong!*'

The single word silenced him.

'You!' Olga pointed to Betty. 'Why are you here?'

Betty blinked. 'Well, my hobby was anthropomorphic taxidermy until the council closed me down. What happened was I used rats to represent people around the town—'

'*Wrong!*'

Olga gradually walked around the room, posing the same question to each participant. They all got the same response from Olga.

'You!' Olga said, pointing her emerald-green forefinger at me. 'Why are you here?'

I'd dreaded this moment because I had no idea what to say. 'She made me come,' I said weakly, indicating Kim. 'It's her fault.'

'Rosie!' Kim said, shocked.

'Wrong!' Olga snapped and turned to Kim. 'And you? Why are you here?'

Kim eyed the old woman for a moment before steeling herself to reply. 'Well, you won the Garibaldi International art prize and—'

As Olga stared at her, her eyes narrowing, Kim faltered. And then—

'Correct!'

A sense of palpable relief rippled across the room as Olga waved at the fruit bowl. 'There are art classes that will teach you how to paint this fruit bowl,' she said. 'That is not this art class.'

Really? I thought. *So why are we here?*

'Any imbecile can learn to paint this in a representational style,' Olga continued. *'Anyone.'*

I studied the apples, oranges, and bananas, certain that my resultant drawing would look nothing like them.

'Art is not about representation,' Olga said. 'If we want to represent it, we need only take a photo. Is that not true? But we want to get a *sense* of the thing. An understanding of what it *truly* is. What lies *beneath* the surface.' She paused. 'On your easel is a charcoal drawing stick and a large drawing pad. Pick up the charcoal and draw the bowl of fruit. You have one minute.'

This was met with complete silence.

'Only o-o-one minute?' Father Tyler stammered. 'To draw the entire bowl of—'

'Fifty-five seconds!'

People snatched up pieces of charcoal and drew.

I stared desperately at my blank sheet, then back at the fruit bowl. *Where do I start?* I carefully started drawing the bowl's bottom edge. No sooner had I reached the part where it angled upwards than our time was up.

'Finish!' Olga commanded. She went around from one person to another. 'Terrible...awful...horrible...' She stopped to examine mine. 'What is that?'

'Uh...the bottom edge of the bowl.'

'It is nothing.'

'No. It's the bottom—'

'It is nothing.'

'Oh.'

Olga continued on to Kim, and her face brightened. 'Yes!' she proclaimed. 'Yes! Everyone! Come and see what Kim has produced.'

Everyone grouped around Kim's easel. Whereas I'd tried drawing one section of the bowl, Kim had run her arm about the page in a series of broad sweeps, coalescing in a clump in the middle. The shape could have been the bowl of fruit. Equally, it might have been a cat with five legs or a bunch of petunias.

'This is what we want,' Olga enthused. 'Kim! You are my star pupil!'

'I'm...' Kim blushed crimson. 'Well, okay.'

'Compare Kim's effort,' Olga said before pointing to my drawing, 'to this!'

Everyone stared at my sketch. I thought my line was rather good, as far as lines went. Although it did look a little like a trainee cartographer's attempt at the Gulf of Mexico.

'This is...*ptah*!' Olga said.

Ptah?

'Everyone!' she declared. 'Return to your easels!

There was a scrambling of feet as everyone scurried back to their places. Kim leaned over. 'Imagine that!' she whispered. 'I'm the star pupil!'

I nodded.

And I'm...ptah?

'Turn your page,' Olga commanded. 'Sixty seconds!'

The charcoal flew.

9

'Wasn't that fun?' Kim said as we walked out into the cold night.

Fun?

'Sure,' I answered. 'If your idea of fun is being terrorised by middle-aged Hungarian women.'

After the one-minute sketches, we'd cut back to forty-five seconds, then thirty seconds. In a countdown to destruction, our final sketches had been only ten seconds each.

'Oh, she's not so bad,' Kim said, airily

'Not so bad?' I stared at her. 'She said my drawings were *ptah*. I think that might mean *spit* in Hungarian. Or vomit. I'm not sure.'

'We've all got to start somewhere.'

Kim was flying high.

I didn't want to puncture her balloon, although I wasn't sure if she was any better than anyone else in the room. By the end of the evening, we had art pads full of charcoal sketches that could have either been fruit bowls or anything else in the known universe.

'And tomorrow night's even better,' Kim enthused. 'We have a live model!'

I nodded absently. 'Well, sure. I've clearly mastered the art of still life. Now to move onto something easy like the *human body.*'

Completely missing my sarcasm, Kim said she'd see me later and walked off into the night. Trixie and I returned to my jeep and were back home within minutes. Nan was still busy knitting outfits for the Zonta club. She offered to make me a cup of tea, but I was exhausted by then.

I climbed into bed and somehow got to sleep. Still, there was no peace to be found in the world of slumber. My dreams were filled with Olga and art classes gone horribly wrong. Every time I would draw something, I'd hear the woman yelling at me.

'Wrong!'

'Wrong!'

'Wrong!'

I woke early the following day to find my hair plastered to my face. 'My goodness,' I muttered. 'That was awful. Why did I sign up for that horrible class?'

After showering, I got dressed and was soon hurrying up the road with Trixie on the way to Cut Rock Lookout. Big, bulbous masses of cloud littered the sky. More rain was on the way, and I didn't mind at all. Cold weather often helped me to think.

A familiar figure leaned against the railing, peering out to sea. It was the same man I'd seen earlier in the week.

'Any whales this morning?' I asked, drawing near.

He turned and grinned. 'No. I'm disappointed. They must all be snoozing.'

'We should probably build some mechanical ones for the tourists,' I said. 'Then everyone gets their photo opportunity.'

Pushing back his unruly red hair, he laughed, and his whole face brightened. 'Duncan Bell,' he said, extending a hand.

'Huh?'

'My name's Duncan Bell.'

'Oh yes!' I said as I struggled to recall my own name. 'Rosie Ryan.'

We shook hands, and it was pleasing to see that his handshake was firm but not too firm. His hands were soft, though I detected one or two callouses.

Manual labour? I pushed the idea from my mind. *Who cares?* This was a nice guy that—now I was looking more closely—was certainly younger than me. It was hard to judge his age. His skin was clear of blemishes, and he could have been five years younger than me. Maybe even ten. It made forty-three-year-old Rosie Ryan feel like a condemned building.

I thought about Vivian and Tony.

Well, it worked for them...

'Feel like a stroll into town?' he asked.

'Why not?' I replied.

Hey, I thought. Even condemned buildings deserve their time in the sun. Don't they? After telling him I was a journalist for the local paper, I asked what he did.

'I'm an actor,' he said as we walked down the hill towards town. 'Which means I'm mostly unemployed and continually searching for work.'

'That's a pretty brave move,' I said. 'Being an actor's a tough job.'

He smiled. 'You have to love the line, *You're not what we're after*, or you'd give up.'

'Would I have seen you in anything?'

It turned out he'd done a few Australian soaps over the years. Not being a soap viewer, I didn't know him, but there were a few commercials too.

'You remember the Victorian tourism ad from last year?' Duncan asked. 'The one where the guy's running down the wharf, sees a pretty girl, and falls into the water?'

I stared at him. 'Hang on. You mean—'

'That was me.'

'That was a *huge* campaign. We even ran a few quarter-page ads from Victorian Tourism. Surely that's enough to make you famous.'

Duncan laughed. 'Not even close,' he said. 'I got a day's pay and an ear infection. You know how many times they had to shoot that scene? Seven. I took antibiotics for a week afterward.'

'The price of fame.'

'You're telling me.'

We'd reached the bottom of the hill, and I was wondering what to do next. Inviting him for coffee seemed too forward. *But I can suggest takeaways.* He agreed to this, and we angled across the road to Sandy's.

'Morning, Rosie,' Sandy said, eyeing me quizzically as she pushed back her cap. I could almost read her mind. She may as well have held up a sign saying *who's this hunky guy?* Somehow, she kept her curiosity in check. 'Are you eating food this morning, or are you strictly on a caffeine diet?'

'Just caffeine for now,' I said. 'Food is overrated.'

Duncan ordered a flat white while I got my usual jumbo double-shot caramel latte. We headed out of the diner together and peered out at the bay. I felt strangely at ease. Maybe it was because there were no expectations. Although he was handsome, Duncan was younger than me, so nothing would ever eventuate.

The big surprise was when he asked for my number.

'So,' I said slowly. 'You're after a guide to show you around town?'

'Something like that. I'm new to Cape Carson, and the only person I know is Mrs Henderson, my eighty-four-year-old landlady. And a journalist is a good friend to have. I'm always after work, and you know lots of people.'

Well, I thought, giving him one of my cards. *At least he's honest.*

A few hours later, I was at my desk working when Ellie Applegate came striding into my office. Jay was out on a job, so she grabbed his seat and glared at me.

'Okay,' she said. 'Spill.'

'Huh?'

'Don't play dumb with me, Rosie Ryan,' she said, grinning as she threw back her dreadlocks. 'Guess what Ralph and I saw as we drove down Percy Street this morning?'

I vaguely remembered an old Volkswagen Kombi heading down the road as I was crossing to Sandy's. 'It wasn't a whale because none were off the coast this morning,' I said.

'Definitely not a whale. More like a nice looking guy walking hand-in-hand with a certain female reporter.'

'*Definitely* not hand-in-hand.'

'*Almost* hand-in-hand,' she amended. 'And the guy?'

I explained that I'd met him up at the lookout, and there was nothing in it: just a friendly guy I happened to stumble across.

'Stumble across?' Ellie said. 'You make him sound like a

rock. Well, if that nice guy happens to ask you on a date, then I think you should say yes.'

'He's quite young.'

'Rosie.' Ellie crossed to the door. 'It's the twenty-first century. Not nineteen-fifty. It's okay to date younger men.'

Hmm.

She left me to get on with my work. As it turned out, I had a busy day. There was a story about new drainage works, another about a wrist watch unearthed beneath one of the town's oldest buildings, and an upcoming photography exhibition at the Lighthouse Inn.

It was early afternoon when a new email pinged into my inbox. Opening it up, I first glanced at it—then stared.

'Okay,' I murmured. 'That's interesting.'

'What is?' Jay asked from his desk. He was rewriting a press release from the local footy club.

'Take a look.'

He hovered over my shoulder as I reread the email:

What makes you think Vivian Shelly was killed by that intruder? She was probably murdered by her scoundrel of a husband. He stands to inherit, you know. Her estate is worth millions.

'What do you make of that?' Jay asked.

'I'm not sure,' I answered as he sat back down. The email service was an anonymous provider operating out of Switzerland. Tracking down the sender was impossible. I filled Jay in briefly about Vivian's murder. 'Her death seems to be a robbery gone wrong.'

'Yeah? You haven't seen *Dial M for Murder*?'

Actually, I had seen *Dial M for Murder*, as I was a huge Hitchcock fan. I knew the story well. A man plans to have his wife murdered by a burglar so he can collect her inheritance. Fortunately, the tables get turned, and the murder doesn't go to plan.

'The killer could have been hired,' I agreed, thinking. 'It wouldn't be the first time someone's hired a hitman.'

I wondered where to start. Speaking to Tony again would be a mistake. If he were guilty, it would only put him on his guard. Interviewing Melissa might point me in the right direction, although I had to be careful about what I said. She could still be loyal to Tony and tip him off. I didn't have contact details for her. Shona at the library might, or she could know someone who did. It only took a few minutes and a couple of phone calls for me to discover that Melissa managed a small motel in Cape Carson. Taking Trixie with me, I decided to drop in unannounced. It was too easy for her to refuse an interview over the phone. Soon, I was pulling into the car park of the Ocean Shores Inn.

There weren't a lot of cars around, which wasn't surprising. This was the quiet season, and it would only get quieter over the next few months. I'd been to the hotel before to interview a visiting band. Although the Ocean Shores was an older place, it had been substantially remodelled over the years and looked good for its age.

I wandered into the foyer and spotted Melissa immediately. She was at the counter handing someone keys for their room.

'Rosie,' she greeted me as soon as the person had left. 'I didn't expect to see you so soon.'

'I get around. How are you coping after Wednesday night?'

Melissa sighed. 'It's all a lot to take in,' she said. 'I knew I'd cause an upset by turning up under a false name. Then there was the séance. And then Vivian was killed by that burglar.'

'You were late joining the séance,' I observed, although I didn't see how this could be relevant to Vivian's death; she died after the séance finished. 'That was a call from your father?'

'Losing mum has been hard on him. I didn't want to hang up when he rang.'

'Did he know about the séance?'

'No. Dad disapproves of that kind of thing.'

'Did you see anything before you came into the Scarlet room? Anything strange near the chapel?'

'The police asked me the same thing. No. I sat down in the living room and chatted to Dad. From where I was, I could see out across the lake. Everything was in darkness other than the lights on the path. The thief didn't come anywhere near the house. The police said he entered via a back lane.'

I nodded, thinking. 'You must be disappointed that you didn't speak with your mum,' I said. 'I suppose it cost a lot to attend the séance?'

'A fortune.' She paused. 'But the money isn't the biggest issue. Vivian could contact the other side. She had some kind of power. I had the chance to speak to my mother, and now that's been taken away—permanently.'

'A lot of people don't believe in spiritualism,' I said. 'Tony never mentioned any trickery on Vivian's part?'

Melissa frowned. 'Tony would never be part of a con. He would never do that. And I know he's devastated by Vivian's death.'

'You've spoken to him?'

'I tried to. I rang up, said a few words, and then Tony hung up on me. Maybe he thinks I want to get back with him, but that isn't why I rang.' She paused. 'Anway, it's over between us. I accept that.'

'Are you seeing anyone?'

'I've dated. But you know something, Rosie? It took me a long time to work this out, but I don't need to be with anyone. I was with Tony for so long that I was locked into the idea of needing to be part of a couple. I don't need to be someone's 'other half'. There's nothing wrong with being solo.'

Everything she was saying made sense. After thanking

Melissa for her time, Trixie and I returned to my jeep. I sat there in silence and thought about what she'd said.

Trixie whined.

'I'm okay, girl,' I said, rubbing the back of her head. 'I'm not upset.'

That was a lie, though. I was upset. Talking to Melissa got me thinking about my grandfather, Frank Ryan. What if it were possible to contact people in the afterlife? Losing Vivian Shelly meant losing that link forever.

Trixie barked.

'All right. I admit it. I'm in a downer. Let's go before I melt into a puddle of tears.'

I headed back into town, grabbed a coffee on my way to the office, and settled down for the rest of the afternoon to complete some stories. The paper was going to print today and, as usual, the atmosphere in the office was slightly chaotic. We either had too much news or not enough of it.

My story about Vivian Shelly took up most of the front page, but there was a last-minute cancellation of an ad from a supplier. This meant we had to write some more copy and fill the remaining gap with photos contributed by the locals.

As Harry always said, the heartbeat of the Cape Carson Gazette was one thing: pictures, pictures, pictures.

The end of the workday meant another night of art with Olga the Barbarian. Would it be any easier tonight? Or another evening of her flying around the classroom on her broomstick while terrorising us lesser mortals?

Trixie and I headed down to the beach. After the rain of the last few days, the afternoon had turned unseasonably warm. It happened sometimes and usually preceded more stormy weather. I sat on one of the benches and watched the waves rolling in.

'How lovely,' I said to Trixie, as she climbed onto the bench and laid her head in my lap. I felt exhausted, and I knew why. I'd been feeling rather emotional all day, and a lot of it was thinking about my grandfather. All this talk of mediums and the afterlife had left me feeling drained. 'Let's just sit for a moment.'

Yawning, I closed my eyes. 'How lovely it is...' I told Trixie. 'Let's just sit...'

Beep!

I blinked. My jaw dropping open, I realised two things at once. The first was that I'd fallen asleep on the bench. The second was that night had fallen, and that meant—

Grabbing out my phone, I read the text message from Kim.

Where are you?!?!? We're starting!!!!!

Letting out a yell, I jumped off the seat, and Trixie broke into a series of frenzied barks as we raced to the car. We piled in, and I drove to the community centre, screeching to a halt outside. Soon, I was staggering in the front door with Trixie at my heel. The class was already underway, with the easels lined up around the room in a semicircle.

Olga glared at me. 'You are late!' she said. 'Great art waits for no one!'

'So sorry,' I mumbled and saw Kim waving frantically from behind an easel on the far end. She must have saved the one beside her for me. 'I had a work emergency, and my cat died—'

Glancing past Olga, I recognised a familiar face.

Huh?

'Hey Rosie,' Duncan said.

The actor lay on a table in front of the easels. My eyes angled down to his bare chest, his stomach, and then—

Good grief!

I careered into Betty Sawyer's easel.

My right foot went under one leg, and I fell, sending the easel flying. It went crashing into the next easel, which belonged to Father Tyler. Like a chain of dominos, the easels went down, sending paint, paper, and brushes everywhere.

The only easel to survive was Kim's, who had dragged it free from the wave of destruction.

I lay hopelessly entangled under the collapsed easel as Olga and the other class members grouped around.

My eyes trailed up Duncan's bare legs.

'Oh,' I said, swallowing. 'Hi.'

10

Nan laughed until she was red in the face. And then she laughed some more.

'One thing about you, Rosie,' she chortled as she lay back on the lounge. 'You certainly know how to make an entrance.'

I scowled. 'I'm glad you find it amusing,' I said. 'Everyone was annoyed. Even Father Tyler—and it's difficult to annoy a priest.'

'That takes effort, I'm sure.'

The class continued after I made my dramatic appearance, but Olga had barely spoken to me. Kim had been supportive, and Duncan—

Well, despite remaining motionless while he modelled, Duncan's eyes had glanced several times in my direction. And I was sure the smirk on his face hadn't been there earlier in the evening. At night's end, I raced out the door without speaking to him and drove home.

After showering and making myself presentable, I'd filled

Nan in on the evening's events. Now we were curled up on the lounge with cups of tea. Besides a sore head, where I'd headbutted the easel, I was physically okay. My reputation as the star reporter for the Cape Carson Gazette was bruised, although my status as a klutz was completely intact.

My phone rang, and it was a number I didn't recognise.

'Hello?'

'Rosie?' A familiar voice said. 'It's Duncan.'

'Oh.' I glanced across at Nan, who was grinning. Snatching up my cup of tea, I escaped to my bedroom, where I could speak in private. 'How are you?'

I sat on my bed as Trixie settled on the floor beside me.

'I'm fine,' Duncan said. 'More's the question, how are you? Are you all right?'

'Oh, I'm okay,' I said, relieved at the concern in his voice. 'A little battered and bruised. There's more damage to my ego than anything else. I'm *very* clumsy sometimes.'

'Everyone has accidents,' he said. 'And seeing me must have come as quite a surprise. I should have told you I was doing some modelling.'

'You did call yourself a jack-of-all-trades,' I answered. 'I expected to see more of you...I mean...I didn't think I'd see that much...that is...'

By now, Duncan was laughing at the other end of the phone. 'I get your meaning,' he said, adding, 'I think. Anyway,

I've supplemented my income over the years with modelling. Sometimes, Rosie, it's life modelling for art studios. It's not that uncommon among actors.'

'Well, you've got the looks for it,' I said and instantly thought it sounded like a come-on. 'I mean...'

'Feel like another coffee some time?' he said, interrupting another round of my illiterate drooling. 'Maybe tomorrow?'

I wasn't sure how to answer. This was all moving a bit fast for me. Duncan seemed like a nice guy, but I didn't want to give him the wrong impression.

'I'm a bit busy,' I said. 'Can I call you, and we'll arrange a time?'

'Sure. Whenever suits.'

Thanking him for calling, I hung up and returned my empty cup to the kitchen. Nan had changed into her nightgown with the words *I'm the Boss* on the back. She was about to head off to bed.

'So,' she said. 'Duncan, eh?'

I groaned. 'He's the model from the art class.'

'Going on a date?'

'Coffee. Maybe. One day.'

'Does Todd know?'

'There's nothing to know!'

To this, she laughed and wished me goodnight.

The next morning, I visited Todd at the police station to

follow up on the case. Constable Jim Turner, staffing the front desk, smiled as I walked in.

'Ah,' he said. 'Mrs Van Gogh.'

'Huh?'

How did he know...

'One of my cousins is doing Olga's class,' he explained. 'He mentioned you. Said something about you falling onto a naked model.'

'I did not fall on a naked model!' I said. 'I tripped and knocked over an easel. Or two. Or three.'

Still grinning, Jim showed me to Todd's office, where the burly sergeant typed two-fingered at his computer. He glanced up from the keyboard as Jim left.

'Try not to knock anything over,' he said. 'The taxpayer pays for all this stuff.'

Groaning, I sat down. 'Has everyone in Cape Carson heard about my little mishap?'

'Not everyone. A few people on Samuel Street don't know. I can tell them if you like—'

'Ha-ha,' I said humourlessly. 'I've got a few questions for you.'

'If it's about male anatomy—'

'It's not,' I firmly assured him. 'It's about the other night. What did you discover about the man who murdered Vivian Shelly?'

'Ah, yes,' Todd said. 'I've got a name: Zane Bennett. He was a mortgage broker. Doesn't have a record, although he has had problems with gambling. I've spoken to his sister, Terri, who says he spent his money as soon as it came in.'

'What sort of gambling?'

'Horse racing, mostly. And one-armed bandits. Apparently, he spent a lot of time at the Smuggler's Inn.'

The Smuggler's Inn was the most disreputable place in town.

'So a mortgage broker decides to rob the home of a noted medium?' I said. 'That seems a little far-fetched.'

'I asked around at the Smuggler's Inn. A few people said that Zane owed money. It could have been to the wrong people. We all do crazy things when we're scared.'

'So his mortgage business wasn't doing well?'

Todd hesitated. 'He was doing okay,' he said. 'According to his sister.'

'So why—'

The sergeant held up a hand. 'One thing I've learned in policing is that not everything gets explained. There are *always* loose ends. Things that don't quite make sense. It doesn't mean we dismiss the most likely explanation just because it doesn't fit our nice neat little story. Zane tried to rob Vivian. The robbery went wrong, and they were both killed.'

'There is another possibility.'

'Which is?'

I thought. 'Well,' I said. 'It's odd that Melissa was late to the séance.'

'I've heard about this already,' Todd said. 'Everyone told me she had a call from her father. It means nothing. I contacted him and confirmed that he rang her. He has some kind of early-onset dementia. Regularity in his routine helps. It's sort of an evening ritual.'

'So there's no connection between Melissa and Zane?'

'None. We've checked his phone records—and hers. Zane lived in Palmdale. Melissa lives in Cape Carson. They didn't know each other.'

'And what about Tony and Zane? Could Tony have had Vivian murdered? Zane could have been paid off.'

Todd rolled his eyes. 'I've checked Tony's phone records too, and there were no calls to Zane.' His gaze settled on me. 'Rosie, the simple explanation is usually the true one. Vivian Shelley died during a bungled robbery. End of story.'

I wasn't ready to give up. 'Well, I'm going to follow up with the other people who attended the séance.'

'Why?'

'There were some odd vibes that night,' I said. 'It was a bit weird.'

'You were there to speak to dead people,' Todd pointed out. 'It's *all* a bit weird.'

'I don't suppose I can get their contact details from you?'

'We don't hand out that kind of information.'

'Todd...'

He smiled. 'But if it's any help, I've already checked, and you can find all those people online,' he said. 'You're the reporter. Do some research.'

'Okay.' I stood up to go. 'Thanks. You've been helpful. Kind of.'

Todd led me through the police station and out onto the street. Dark clouds had gathered during the morning, and a storm was coming. It would probably rain within the hour.

'So, how are things going with Duncan?' Todd asked.

'You know his name?'

'News travels fast in Cape Carson.'

'I barely know the guy,' I said, glaring at him. 'How are things with you and Yvonne?'

'I told you we're old friends. Why do you ask?'

'I'm a reporter,' I said. 'I get paid to be curious.'

11

'Looks like this is the place,' I said to Kim.

It was late in the day, and Kim had taken the afternoon off from work. I'd been able to locate Alicia and Russell's home through a website for his business. It turned out he was an accountant in a nearby town called Hasset. Russell's business was run from his home, a quarter-acre block half a kilometre from the town centre. The sign reading *Warren Accounting* was blowing wildly in the breeze as we pulled into the drive-way.

The storm had been chasing us inland all the way from Cape Carson. Forked lightning danced between the clouds, and thunder rumbled ominously. Some kangaroos watched from a nearby paddock as we hurried to the front door. I glanced back at the heaving sky as I knocked. 'I hope Alicia and Russell let us in,' I said. 'This is a long way to travel to get caught in the rain.'

'Looks like it's here,' Kim announced as big drops started

staining the footpath grey.

The door swung open and Alicia appeared. 'My goodness,' she said. 'It's Rosie and Kim. What a surprise! And a lovely dog.'

I introduced Trixie. 'Do you mind if we come in, Alicia?' I asked, indicating the tumbling rain. 'I'd like to ask a couple of questions—if you have time.'

The woman showed us into a snug reception room. It had once been a hallway, but a simple timber counter had been built with a few chairs positioned opposite. Smiling, Alicia patted Trixie's head.

'What a beautiful dog,' she said. 'I don't own a dog, but if I did own one, it would be a beagle.'

'They're a friendly breed,' I said.

Russell limped into the room clutching his walking stick. 'Hello,' he said, frowning. 'What brings you ladies out here?'

'I was hoping to ask a few questions about the other night,' I said.

'I suppose that's okay,' Russell said. 'As long as it doesn't take long. We're expecting a call from a client.'

We filed after them into Russell's office, a snug room at the front of the house, and sat around his desk. A picture window looked out onto the yard. The rain was really coming down now, and I was glad we weren't driving in it.

'Please don't use our names,' Alicia said. 'We want that now more than ever.'

'Your names won't be used,' I promised. 'But I'm wondering what you mean by *now more than ever*.'

'My mind is at ease now.' Alicia sunk her hands into her lap. 'I've spoken to Dad, and he said he was all right. There was no ill-treatment at the nursing home.'

'Alicia's father, Gideon, is with his brothers,' Russell added, eyeing his wife. 'Both Bill and Terry. They're all at peace.'

I wondered exactly who he was trying to convince: himself or Alicia.

'I'm pleased you're so positive about the séance,' I said. 'What happened later was awful.'

'A terrible shock,' Alicia agreed thoughtfully. 'And Vivian had so much to give the world.'

Russell remained silent. I glanced over at Kim, who was frowning; she was having the same reservations about him too.

'Zane Bennett was the man who killed Vivian,' Kim said. 'You've never heard of him?'

Both Alicia and Russell shook their heads. 'No,' Russell said. 'Should we?'

'We're just curious if he knew anyone else who was there that night,' I said.

'We'd remember if we knew him,' Alicia said.

'He isn't one of your clients?'

'Absolutely not,' Russell replied.

The rain began to pound even harder. Thunder rumbled, the distant hills disappeared, and then the nearest fields slid behind a wall of rain. A phone rang in another room.

'Alicia,' Russell said. 'Will you get that please? It must be Somchai.'

Nodding, she got up and departed through the doorway. No sooner was she gone than Russell leaned forward, anger in his eyes.

'I'm not sure what it is that you women want,' he said. 'But Alicia's been through enough. She doesn't need—'

'You're sure that Vivian was a fraud,' I said.

'A fraud?' he said, taken aback. 'Well, I'm not sure—'

'I agree that Alicia believes, and that's what matters in the end. Her peace of mind must be worth it.' I stared him down. 'But you know the truth.'

Kim spoke up. 'It's William,' she said. 'Isn't it?'

I nodded. She'd noticed, too.

'During the séance,' Kim continued, 'Vivian said that Gideon was with his brothers William and Terry. It seemed strange. Most Williams are called Bill. Or Will. Not all of them. But most.'

'And just now, you called him Bill,' I added. 'You know—or suspect—that Vivian was a fake.'

Russell fell back in his chair and peered out at the torrential rain. 'It cost us a lot of money to see Vivian,' he said. 'I was dead-set against it, of course. It's all a load of hogwash. I didn't believe it for a second, but Alicia was sure her father was badly treated at the nursing home. She was on about it all day and night. I couldn't take it any longer.

'I thought that if we went, it might give her peace of mind.' He leaned forward and lowered his voice. 'And it has. She's a different woman. Alicia's looking forward to life. For the first time in a long time, I can see some light at the end of the tunnel.'

'And the reference to William?' I asked.

'There's a memorial page for Gideon,' Russell said, peering into the distance. 'Bill is referred to as William on there. No one ever called him William. He didn't even call himself that. I guess Vivian trawled the internet for information about families and those who have died. She used that information during the séance.' He shook his head. 'The whole thing was a scam. I'm sure of it.'

I had to raise another issue too. A lot of information can be found on the internet. Sometimes more than people wanted. 'You had your own history with Vivian,' I said. Russell didn't speak, so I nodded to his cane. 'You were in an accident several years ago. At the time, you were working for a construction company. A vehicle slid on wet roads and slammed into your truck. It was quite a mess. A couple of guys were injured, including yourself. You spent a long time in hospital. Would you care to tell us about that?'

The accountant rubbed his leg. 'Accidents happen,' he said. 'I don't blame anyone for that.'

'Even if Vivian was the driver?'

Russell pursed his lips.

'I read the reports about the accident,' I continued. 'It was serious. Vivian wasn't to blame. Or, at least, that's what the police decided. She hadn't been drinking. The worst she was guilty of was speeding.' I nodded to the rain falling heavily outside. 'Everyone gets told to slow down on wet roads. The police weren't able to ascertain the cause of the accident. And according to Vivian, she hit an oil patch on the wet road and skidded. You spent months in hospital. At one time, they thought you might not walk again.'

'There was damage to my spine,' Russell confirmed without looking at us. 'But I recovered. It took time. I still use the stick, but I'm grateful I can walk. Another inch to the left, I would have been confined to a wheelchair. It was twenty years ago. Another life. It all happened before I met Alicia.'

'Vivian may not have made the connection between you and the men injured in that accident,' I said. 'Your surname has changed since then.'

'There's nothing suspicious about that. I reverted back to my mother's maiden name after my stepfather died. He was an abusive man. I didn't want to share his name.'

Kim spoke up. 'You must feel furious about the accident,' she said. 'Anyone would feel angry at the person who almost killed them.'

Russell grimaced. 'You're right,' he said evenly. 'I did feel angry. But it was a long time ago. Wounds heal.'

'They must have healed beautifully. There are mediums all around the country, and yet you used Vivian.'

'She was the best.' Russell almost spat the words. 'Alicia didn't know that Vivian caused the accident. All she knew was that Vivian Shelly was the best. So we went to see her.' He scowled. 'Is there a point to these questions?'

'Only that you had a good reason to want Vivian dead.'

'That's ridiculous. Besides,' he added, 'I was in the séance when Vivian was murdered.'

'You could have hired Zane to kill her.'

'For that matter,' Russell said, 'anyone could have hired him. I imagine Vivian Shelly had many enemies. I'm sure a lot of people wanted her dead.' He shook his head. 'But seeing her has helped Alicia. I can't deny that. And maybe there is some justice in this world. Alicia's at peace, and that's what matters.'

There was the clattering of Alicia's shoes in the hallway.

Russell's face twisted with anguish. 'Don't tell Alicia,' he urged. '*Please.*'

Alicia entered the room. 'That was Somchai,' she said. 'What a chatterbox. He's setting up that trust fund. Took him long enough to decide.' Her eyes crossed from Russell to us. 'Everything okay?'

No one spoke at first. Then I nodded. 'It's fine,' I said and turned to Kim. 'I think we've got everything we need.'

'Sure have,' she agreed.

Everyone stood. Russell and Alicia saw us out to the front yard. Although the clouds were still threatening, the rain had stopped. The sun was beaming through a hole in the cloud cover, sending a jagged spotlight across the distant hills.

'Thanks for dropping by,' Alicia said.

'Yeah, thanks,' Russell added.

'It's a tragedy about Vivian,' Alicia continued. 'But she's on the other side now. As she told us, it's a place of peace. There's nothing to worry about.'

'That's right,' I said. 'There's nothing to worry about.'

12

'We can't know for sure,' Kim said. 'But it looks like Vivian was a fraud.'

The rain had started again and was falling solidly. My eyes were fixed on the wet roads as we manoeuvred through the countryside. Rolling grassy hills stretched away to the horizon where lightning carved broken shards into the charcoal-grey sky.

'It seems that way,' I said. 'The question is—did Tony know? Or was he fooled too?'

Kim peered out at the pouring rain. 'And if he did know, would he spill the beans?'

'There's a lot of money in that business. That house is worth millions. I think he'd stay quiet.' I aimed the car around a bend. 'But this doesn't get us any closer to who murdered Vivian. Whether she was a fraud or not, Zane murdered her. He either did it as part of a bungled robbery—'

'Or someone paid him to do it.'

I glanced at my watch. It was after lunch, and I was feeling hungry. We drove through the relentless rain, finally stopping at a tiny café in a small town. The woman running the place was glad of our business; we were probably her first customers for hours. After some cheese and tomato sandwiches, and coffee that left much to be desired, we hit the road again. Fortunately, I had another contact we could visit before the day was through.

Edwina Parkridge's home was a tidy place near the back of Cape Carson, where the town met the bush. It was in a lovely location, marred only by the water tower at the end of her street. It was a terrible eyesore.

The colossal concrete cylinder had been installed decades before and could be spotted halfway across town.

Her lawn was impeccable, with rose bushes lined up across the front of the yard behind the white picket fence. A pair of bushes, shaped into giant hearts, dominated the yard, one on each side of the straight footpath that led to the front door.

'Topiary,' I said, shuddering. 'I've never been able to stand it.'

'Me neither,' Kim agreed. 'All that neatness. Just...creepy.'

We took Trixie with us to the front door and pressed the doorbell. It played a few notes from Chopin's Funeral March.

Kim and I exchanged glances.

She shook her head. 'And you think I'm weird.'

The door flew open, and Edwina appeared. 'My goodness!' she said. 'It's Rosie and Kim! And who's this little one?'

Her attention had shot to Trixie. I introduced them, and the stout woman gave Trixie a quick pat on the head.

'What a beautiful dog!' she enthused. 'I used to own a dog. His name was Andrew. He's with my sister and parents in heaven now. Nothing lasts forever.' She straightened up. 'But what brings you girls here?'

'We're after some more information for the story we're doing on Vivian. If you could spare us a few minutes...'

'Of course!' she said, inviting us in. 'Welcome to my humble home!'

Humble was what the house was not. The interior décor could best be described as Spiritual Crystal because both concepts dominated the home. A half-life-sized statue of Jesus filled the hallway. The benevolent saviour with arms spread, hands open, smiled kindly at us as we passed. Beside him was a Buddha, and beside him what appeared to be a Hindu God riding a parrot.

The sideboard in the living room was full of crystals and semi-precious stones. Clouds had been painted on the walls in the living room. An enormous eye covered the ceiling. Green, pink and orange neon signs nestled among the clouds with various messages: *Love, See Through the Curtain* and *I'm a Believer*. A water fountain in the shape of a rainbow gurgled happily in the corner.

Among all this lounged a squadron of cats. They sat about on sofas, tables and sideboards. There were at least a dozen. Probably more.

'Don't mind my little family,' Edwina said. 'I love my cats though they do get underfoot.'

'This is...amazing,' I said.

'I know,' Edwina said, nodding with approval. 'I can feel Gretchen and all those who have gone before. Oh, I'm not a medium. I'm not blessed with that ability. Still, the curtain between our world and the next is so thin that I feel their presence.' She focused on us. 'Do you girls ever feel that?'

'My grandfather died a few years back,' I said, feeling strangely choked up as I said it. 'My grandmother senses his presence.'

'Those who are gone are still with us.'

I cast my gaze across the room. Everything either sparkled or glowed. Edwina certainly had her own style. 'We'd like to ask you about the other night,' I said. 'Specifically about the man who murdered Vivian.' Edwina invited us to sit, and I planted myself beside a cushion that had a rainbow embroidered across it that said *Beyond*. 'The man's name was Zane Bennett. Does that ring a bell?'

Edwina frowned. 'Zane?' she said. 'I've never known anyone of that name.'

'You mentioned you and Gretchen used to go bowling. Could you have known him from bowling?'

The frown deepened. 'Not at all. I hope you're not suggesting that I had anything to do with Vivian's death?'

'Not at all,' Kim said. 'We're just wondering if anyone had a connection with him, no matter how slight.'

Edwina shook her head.

'Were you happy with Vivian's reading?' I asked.

'Very. I've even ordered the video of the night.'

'A video's available?'

'The link is being sent out,' Edwina said. 'It should have arrived by now, but it's probably been delayed because of what happened to Vivian.'

I nodded. Here was yet another income stream for Vivian and Tony. Everything about this business generated money. I glanced about the room. A bookcase faced onto a sunroom.

'You've got Vivian's books?' I said.

'Every last one of them.'

'You didn't get her to sign them?'

'No. She's signed them before.'

'So you've met previously.'

'A few times. I'm not sure if Vivian remembered me or not. I've been to see a lot of mediums. None were like Vivian.' Edwina sighed. 'Her loss is a tragedy, although I suppose she's with family now.'

'You seemed quite satisfied after you spoke to Gretchen.'

'Speaking to my sister always sets me at ease.'

'It was an emotional evening,' I said carefully. 'I noticed you looked a little...shaken...after you'd spoken to her.'

Edwina swallowed. 'It was the bridge. The atmosphere is...charged sometimes when the curtain is thin. That's what we felt.'

'I felt that too,' Kim offered. 'Although, the look on your face—'

'It was nothing.'

The woman's hands were clenched, her mouth pursed.

She saw something, I thought. *Or heard something?*

What is she not telling us?

'Did Tony do something that worried you?' I asked. 'Or did you notice something—'

Edwina's face fell. 'My goodness,' she said. 'Look at the time. I didn't realise it was so late. I must ask you girls to leave.'

'If you saw something unethical—' Kim began.

'Really,' Edwina said, standing. 'You have to go.'

Smiling reassuringly, I got up, and Kim followed my lead. I complimented Edwina again on her house as we went to the front door, though she didn't reply. She uttered a quick goodbye before firmly closing the door behind us.

'What happened there?' Kim asked as soon as we were back in the car.

I slipped Trixie a doggy snack. 'I don't know,' I confessed. 'She saw something the other night. Something wrong. I don't know what.'

'Was she looking at anyone in particular?'

'Not that I recall. It was after Vivian spoke to Alicia and Sidney. She then moved onto the people who were live-streaming.'

'Do you remember their names?'

I thought. 'There was a Rachel,' I said. 'Someone named John.'

I closed my eyes and tried to remember the events of the night. It was hard to focus. The atmosphere had felt so charged. It was hard to put it all together. 'Spirits' had spoken to most of the participants: Alicia and Russell, Sidney, Edwina, and Tania. Kim and I had been left out. So had Melissa.

What did Edwina see?

We drove back to town. Dropping Kim off at her work, I returned to the office with Trixie. The weather had turned windy, and a brisk onshore breeze was pushing in from the west. I had just stomped in through the front door when Harry called from his office.

I stuck my head in the door. 'It's Saturday,' I said. 'Don't you have a life?'

'Keeping the paper afloat is my life,' Harry said, grinning. 'What brings you in?'

'Following up on a story.'

'Interested in another one? A robbery at the art gallery?'

'What? Someone stole some paintings?'

'No. Books from the collection.'

Like many art galleries, the Cape Carson Art Centre had a library of books related to art and artists.

'So we're investigating stolen books?' I said. 'That's big news now?'

'We're in Cape Carson,' he said. 'Big news is whatever we can find.' He thought. 'Wait a minute. Have you contacted Charlie Holmes about his totems?'

'Not exactly.'

'Does that mean *no*?'

'I promise I'll contact him.'

The Art Centre was on William Street. Within minutes I was making my way in through the entrance. The front of the building was a federation-style home built around nineteen hundred. This housed a lot of the early Australian collection. A vast extension had been added to the rear in the early nineteen nineties. The new section had high ceilings, and skylights, and could accommodate hundreds of paintings.

A few minutes later, Trixie and I were in Simon Trinn's office. The director was a skinny man with curly red hair and an easy smile. I'd interviewed him several times over the years.

'It's the strangest robbery,' he said. 'And we've had some

strange robberies.'

He wasn't wrong about that. There had been some strange crimes at the art gallery over the years, including the theft of a fish tank from the foyer leading into the building. The thief had assumed it to be an avant-garde art piece and had tried to ransom it for one hundred thousand dollars. Simon Trinn responded by saying they could keep it, and that Mona, the goldfish in the tank, had to be fed three times a day and to change the water once a week.

The fish tank—complete with Mona—was returned the following day.

Simon took me to the reading room, a square chamber with high shelves.

A solitary window illuminated an oak table surrounded by timber chairs. 'Anyone can come here. We have a few thousand books, with a particular emphasis on Australian artists.'

I glanced about. 'So what books were taken?'

'Our whole section on Olga Farago.'

'Really?' I said, staring at him. 'Anything else?'

'Not that we can tell.' Simon pointed to a gap on the shelves. 'Mind you, we didn't have a lot of books about her. Only about four. They're all gone.'

I thought about the people attending Olga's classes: Father Tyler, Betty, and the others. There had been a lot of excitement around Olga teaching the class. Could someone have stolen the books to copy her style? To be in her favour?

'Can you describe the person who took them?' I asked.

'Unfortunately not. We had a work experience student manning the front desk. She didn't take much notice of the person. Apparently they were of average height, had a big coat, a scarf, and a hat. They couldn't make out their face.'

'Their voice?'

'Could have been a man or a woman.'

My goodness, I thought. *This is a real mystery.*

'Was there anything special about those books? Besides them being about Olga's artwork?'

'Not that I know.'

'They're not signed first editions? Nothing like that?'

Simon shook his head. 'I have no idea why anyone would have taken them,' he said. 'They don't have any special value, as far as I can tell. Olga was big in her day. Her web installations were ground-breaking. These days, a lot of people have forgotten about her. She's been out of vogue for several years.'

After taking a few photos of the room, I returned to the car with Trixie.

'How's that?' I said to her. 'Someone obviously likes her art.'

Trixie covered her face with her paws.

'Yep,' I agreed. 'Me neither.'

13

'This is the place,' I said.

I pulled my jeep into the driveway of Tania Knight's home. The place was a rundown farm in the heart of the country, about fifty kilometres northwest of Cape Carson. The fields were overgrown. A barn beside the house had collapsed in a heap. A windmill had snapped in half.

Kim peered across the neglected paddocks. 'Something tells me Tania's not a farmer,' she said.

'It's not her strong point.'

Even the yard adjoining the house looked forgotten. An enormous patch of thistle had swallowed the lawn completely. Weeds grew through breaks in the paving stones. The rusting wire fence was leaning so badly it looked ready to fall over.

I recognised the car in the driveway. The dusty old Holden had been parked outside Vivian's house the night she died. We crossed to the front door, and knocked. There was no answer for so long that I thought Tania was out. Then there was the sound of shuffling feet from inside, and the door eased open.

Tania appeared. Her hair was in disarray, and she wore a lilac dressing gown. I reminded myself that it was mid-afternoon.

'Oh,' Tania said. 'This is a surprise.'

'I'm sorry to call like this.' Clearly, some tact was required. 'I'm finishing my article, and I was hoping you could answer a couple of questions.'

'I'm busy right now.'

'It will only take a minute.'

Tania looked like she wanted to kick us off her property. She glanced inside before nodding to an outdoor garden set. 'We can sit over there,' she said. 'But this can't take long. I've got to be somewhere.'

Sitting on the peeling metal furniture, I took out a notepad and pen. I was about to ask my first question when I looked closer at Tania. Beneath her nightgown, she wore an old X-Files t-shirt that read *The Truth is Out There*. Noticing my gaze, Tania pulled her nightgown tighter before taking out a packet of cigarettes and lighting up.

'What do you want to know?' she asked.

'I hope you don't mind,' I began. 'I read your website.'

She shrugged. 'That's why it's there.'

'It was harrowing reading about Peter,' I said. Peter Knight had been holidaying with his mother on the south coast of New South Wales. They'd visited a local beach which had appeared calm. What Tania hadn't known was that a rip had already dragged a few swimmers out earlier that day. They'd only survived by swimming parallel with the beach and angling to shore further down the coast.

The rip was even worse when Peter and Tania went out to swim. She'd lost sight of her son, and he'd been dragged out to sea and disappeared in the foamy breakwater. His body had been found later that day. 'It must have been terribly traumatic for you.'

Tania puffed nervously on her cigarette. 'It was a shock,' she said. 'A total, mind-numbing shock. You really can't imagine what it's like. One moment everything's fine. It's a beautiful day at the beach. You're looking ahead to the future. Then your entire world turns upside down. I kept my eyes on Peter the whole time. I turned away for a few seconds. When I looked back, he was gone.'

'You work in advertising?' Kim asked.

The woman's eyes narrowed. 'Yes,' she said. 'What of it?'

She may have thought we had a poor impression of advertising and people who worked in that industry. 'Nothing,' I said quickly. 'How long have you lived here?'

'Not long. About six months.' She paused. 'I left my job after Peter died. It's been quite a hard time.'

'What brought you to Vivian's séance?' I asked. 'Were you a believer...'

'In the supernatural?' Tania scoffed. 'Not at all. But I was desperate to contact Peter because I felt guilty about what had happened. Was the accident my fault? Should I have done more? I needed answers.'

'And did you get them?'

Tania glanced away. 'I got some resolution.'

Something approaching a smirk played at the edge of her mouth. *What is happening here?* I had the distinct impression that she was toying with us. I glanced at Kim, who had the slightest frown on her forehead. She obviously thought something was odd too.

'Do you believe you spoke to your son?' Kim asked.

Tania stared at us. 'Oh yes,' she said, finally. 'I spoke to Peter. It was comforting. Up until the séance, I was unable to sleep. I couldn't get closure to my life. Now I feel as if I can move on.' She glanced at her watch. 'Talking about moving on, I have to get going. I've got to meet someone.'

'Of course,' I said.

She shepherded us to the front gate, said a quick *goodbye*, and hurried back into her house. Kim and I didn't speak until we reached the car.

'She's an odd woman,' Kim said.

'Something's up,' I said. 'Something very strange.'

I started the car and drove down the road. After a moment, I pulled over to the side.

'What are you doing?' Kim asked.

'Tania said she had to meet someone. We'll see if she was telling the truth.'

We didn't have long to wait. Less than ten minutes later, Tania's old Holden came trundling out. 'Not wearing her dressing gown now,' I observed.

We ducked as she passed by.

'I wonder where she's headed,' Kim said.

'Let's find out.'

We waited a minute before trailing after her.

Staying at a distance, we followed her onto Terang Road. It turned on Ararat Road, and for the next hour, we stayed several hundred metres behind. Open countryside gradually surrendered to the town of Ararat, and we passed long straight streets of single-storey homes before reaching the middle of town.

Here, Tania turned left, and parked in a forty-five-degree angle spot. We drove for another half a block before stopping and getting out of the jeep. There was no sign of Tania.

'Where's she gone?' Kim hissed.

'I don't know.'

Crossing the road, we slowly made our way down, keeping our eyes peeled.

'This is why we need disguises,' Kim muttered.

I groaned. 'Kim,' I said. 'Really? Disguises? What do we

pack? Emergency moustaches? Wigs?'

'It's not such a crazy idea. They might not work if we meet someone face-to-face—'

'They would *never* work if we met someone face-to-face.'

'—but they *would* give us an advantage at a distance,' she said, not ready to surrender the idea. 'All we can do right now is limp.'

'We could wear a parrot on a shoulder. Or an eyepatch. Maybe even a scar.'

'You're not taking my idea seriously.'

'We are not wearing disguises.'

'Well,' Kim said, annoyed. 'I'm limping. And I suggest you stoop. It's like walking down the street with a Harlem Globetrotter.'

'I'm not stooping! I stooped right through high school—'

'So it worked!'

'At least I'm not hobbit-sized!'

'I am not a hobbit!'

Just as Kim's status as a hobbit seemed ready to erupt into a full-blown argument, she grabbed my arm and pointed. 'Look!' she hissed. 'Tania's in that café!'

We hid behind a van.

Tania was sitting in the front window of a small place called The Spot. She was in an animated conversation with a well-dressed man who wore a sports jacket and tie. The man was square-jawed with black-rimmed glasses.

Tania was shaking her head while the man listened intently.

'I wonder what they're talking about,' I pondered.

'We could get closer if we had disguises,' Kim complained stubbornly.

'What are you doing?'

Kim and I jumped. A teenage girl with an auburn ponytail and narrow eyes was standing behind us.

'Uh,' I said. 'Nothing.'

'Are you detectives?' she asked.

'No, we're just—'

'Yes!' Kim intervened. 'We're detectives. And we need some help. Will you help us?'

The girl grinned. 'You bet I can! I've always wanted to be a detective.'

'What's your name?' I asked.

'Marilyn.'

'Fantastic. What we need—'

'But it'll cost you.'

I glared. 'Really?' I said. 'Didn't you always want to be a detective?'

'Sure,' Marilyn said. 'But I want to be rich too.'

My jaw clenched. I gave the brat ten dollars and said I wanted to know what Tania and the man were discussing.

'No worries. My mum owns the café. I can go in and hang

around. Give me a few minutes.'

Marilyn crossed the road and went inside. Fifteen minutes passed slowly as we watched the conversation from a distance. Finally, just as I thought Marilyn had escaped through the café's back door, she came scooting out and crossed the road to us.

'Wow,' she said, drawing near. 'You'll never guess what they were talking about.'

'What?' I asked.

'Well,' Marilyn said. 'It's ten dollars to get me to listen. It's another ten for me to tell you.'

I turned to Kim. 'Murder *is* illegal,' I said. 'Isn't it? Please tell me it's not.'

'Not if there are mitigating circumstances,' she advised me but handed another ten dollars to the young blackmailer.

Marilyn huddled close. 'I couldn't hear a lot,' she said. 'But they were talking about a book.'

'A book? What book?' I asked.

'Not one that you can buy. It hasn't been published yet. The woman wants to publish it. She's arguing with the man about how much she should get.'

I peered out from behind the van again. Tania and the man were exiting the café. He led her towards his car, a late-model Audi. I took out my phone and snapped a few pictures. I checked them. At this distance, the images weren't great, but they would do. The pair spoke for another minute before the man said goodbye and drove off. Tania returned to her car and did the same.

We thanked Marilyn and thoughtfully headed back to my jeep.

'What do you make of all that?' I asked as we climbed in.

'I don't know if Marilyn's ever going to be a detective,' Kim said. 'But being an extortionist seems likely. As far as the conversation goes, it sounds like Tania's trying to make it as an author.'

I started the engine. 'An autobiography about losing her son?'

'Could be. Would a publisher be interested in that?'

'I don't know.'

We drove away, leaving the town behind, and cut through the countryside. It was late afternoon, the horizon was clear, and the sky was a solid sheet of cerulean blue.

Although everything looked fine, I knew appearances could be deceiving; storms lay ahead.

14

'So, how was last night's art class?' Nan asked as she sipped her morning tea.

'It's hard to put it into words,' I said. 'Something between awful and horrendous.'

'That bad?'

'Worse.'

I gazed across the backyard where big eucalyptus trees frowned across the lawn. A crow gave a mournful cry from its position balanced on a side fence. I took a mouthful of tea.

'Kim's quite a good artist,' I told Nan. 'Most of the others are good too. I seem to be the only klutz who can't draw or paint. We were sketching a bust of Julius Caesar last night. My picture looked like he'd been run over by a bus.'

'You can't be perfect at everything.'

'I'm not perfect at anything,' I laughed. 'But I try.'

My phone buzzed as a message appeared: Harry. I read through it—and groaned. 'Harry wants me to check out a bin that was set alight yesterday,' I said. 'It was behind the Chinese restaurant.'

'Vandalism?'

'Looks that way.' I shook my head. 'This is a big step down from interviewing movie stars and celebrities.'

Nan snorted. 'There's a price for living in paradise.'

'And what are you doing today?'

'More outfits for the premmie babies. We've got several dozen ready now.'

I took Nan's hand. 'Has anyone ever told you how fantastic you are?' I asked.

Nan laughed. 'Dave does all the time,' she said. 'He's a good man.'

'He's got good taste,' I told her.

I was already dressed for the day, so I finished my tea and headed off with Trixie. We drove down to William Street, where I parked. The Percy Street shops backed onto this street, and this whole stretch of road was an eyesore. The backyards of the shops were unsightly, with rubbish bins lining the street.

'Not the prettiest spot in Cape Carson,' I said to Trixie.

She barked.

After reaching the back of the Imperial Chinese restaurant, it only took a second to identify the vandalised bin. It lay in a molten mess beside the footpath. Robert Li, the owner, was taking empty boxes out the back. He gave me a wave and angled over.

'Hey Rosie,' he said. 'You heard about our bin?'

'Harry told me.' I critically examined the pile of goo. 'Did you see or hear anyone?'

'No, and it wasn't even dark. It's usually drunks from the pub who think it's funny setting bins alight.'

I inhaled. The fire was long gone, but I was sure I could smell kerosene. 'This is a serious fire,' I said. 'What was in the bin?'

'Cardboard waste.'

Poking among the debris, I found scraps of food boxes and old menus, although a few sheets of paper seemed to have escaped the blaze. 'These are from a book,' I said. 'Did you throw any books away?'

Robert raised an eyebrow. 'Rosie,' he said. 'Growing up in the Li household, burning books was a capital offence.'

I looked closely at a page and saw an abstract splash of colour.

What on Earth...

'This is from the art centre,' I muttered.

Robert peered over my shoulder. 'Really?'

I explained the books had been stolen from the Cape Carson Art Centre. 'Do you have security cameras?' I asked. 'I'd love to track down the culprit.'

Robert shook his head. 'Sorry, Rosie,' he said. 'No cameras. Maybe one of the other businesses?'

A mixture of businesses and homes lined the other side of the road. Thanking Robert, I asked him to keep the details of the burnt books to himself. Then I started door-knocking, asking if anyone had a video showing the backs of the shops. It took half an hour, but I finally came across a homeowner named Jolene who had a camera installed.

The young mother had a struggling toddler in her arms. 'I had the camera put in when my ex-husband was calling at all hours,' she said. 'I eventually had a restraining order taken out. That was over a year ago.'

'The camera's still working?' I asked.

'I haven't checked it for months. It should still be okay.'

She promised to upload the footage to the net and send me a link. Ten minutes later, I was stumbling through the door of Sandy's. The buxom owner was behind the counter making coffee.

'Help,' I groaned. 'I need caffeine.'

Sandy grinned. 'I can tell,' she said. 'It is takeaway?'

Nodding, I grabbed a seat in the window while I waited. Reading through my phone, I glanced up to see Duncan passing. The handsome actor tossed back his red hair as he stuck his head in the door.

'Got time for a chat?' he asked.

'Sure.' I asked if he wanted to join me for coffee, but he said he could only stay for a moment.

'I've got a video call in half an hour,' he said. 'An audition.'

'What's the role?'

'Hamlet.'

'You'd be playing him?'

Duncan lowered his voice dramatically. '*To die, to sleep—To sleep, perchance to dream.*' He smiled. 'What do you think?'

'Hey,' I said, impressed. 'Pretty good.'

'Let's hope the producers think so. Be good if it happens. The show is a modern reinterpretation at the Melbourne Art Centre. A zombie version.'

I raised an eyebrow. 'A *zombie* version?' I said. 'You mean that undiscovered country from where no traveller returns?'

'Hey! You know your Shakespeare!'

'A line here and there.'

Sandy brought my coffee over, and I went outside with Duncan. He asked how the art classes were proceeding.

'Only two more nights. Then I can resume my normal life!'

'That bad, huh?'

'My skill set does not include painting and drawing.'

'Well, you're clearly a writer.'

'There's no clearly about it,' I said.

'You've never tried writing a novel?'

'Sure. Several. They never go anywhere.'

'Well, you know the old saying, Rosie. If at first, you don't succeed...'

'—try, try again?'

Duncan grinned. 'You got it.'

He wished me a good day, and I watched him as he walked down the street and out of sight. Trixie nuzzled my leg. 'Yes, I know, girl,' I said. 'He's handsome and all, but what about Todd?'

Trixie barked.

'Shakespeare was right,' I sighed. 'The course of true love never did run smooth.'

We returned to the car, and I drove around to the office. There, I typed up my notes about what I'd discovered so far about Vivian's death and the burnt books. An email arrived from Jolene with a link to the video footage. I started trawling through, but it only took a minute to realise the footage was useless. It only showed the street outside her home. The other side of the road lay in darkness.

Jay came stumbling into the office.

'What are you doing here?' I asked.

'My internet connection at home has gone down, and I need to send my auntie some pictures for Aryan's funeral.'

'How is all that going?'

'It'll be a big event,' he said. 'Indian funerals always are. At least it's a good opportunity to get the family together.' He nodded to my computer. 'What are you working on?'

I told him about the vandalism at the art centre. 'It's quite a mystery,' I said. 'Why would someone burn books?'

Jay sighed. 'That question's been asked for centuries,' he said. 'Is Olga likable?'

'About as likable as a lion with a sore toe.'

'Then maybe it's a personal vendetta.'

I thought about the people in my class: Samantha, Father Tyler, Betty, and the others. Could one of them dislike the woman so much that they'd destroy her books? Olga had been problematic from the beginning. She had only one favourite, and that was Kim.

My phone buzzed as a message arrived.

Ha, I thought. *Speak of the devil…*

I read the message from Kim:

Let me know what's happening. Are we tracking down any killers today?

I rang her back.

'I was just thinking about you,' I said.

'Good thoughts, I hope.'

'Absolutely. Except I'm jealous of your drawing skills.'

'Don't be so hard on yourself. I liked your sketch of Julius Caesar.'

'Although, he did look like he'd been hit by a bus. Or a chariot, as the case may be.' I glanced through my contacts. 'As far as interviewing suspects go, we still haven't spoken to Sidney Langston. He lives in a house on the Great Coastal

Road.'

'Great. I can take some time off from here. Can you pick me up?'

I gave Kim an enthusiastic *yes* and hung up. Soon, Kim, Trixie, and I were heading east along the Coastal Road. Although the wind had picked up, it was a glorious day. Cream-tipped waves spread across the ocean as far as the eye could see.

I smiled. 'What a terrible place to live,' I said to Kim.

'Positively awful,' she agreed, grinning. 'I don't know how we cope. Maybe we—hey! Stop! There's a whale!'

She pointed into the distance. One of the road's many lookouts was ahead, so I slowed and pulled in. We climbed out into the freezing wind. Despite my shivering, I didn't mind as I gazed out to sea. Kim was right. More than right, actually, as a breaching whale was quickly followed by two more.

Kim and I leaned on the fence and watched as a water spray erupted from a whale's blowhole. I felt like jumping for joy. It was a glorious image. Whales were hunted almost to extinction until whaling was made illegal back in the nineteen-thirties.

Since then, the number of Southern Right whales had gradually increased.

I shook my head.

How could anyone harm such graceful creatures?

Kim nudged me, grinning. I tried to think of something

profound to say but came up with nothing. Some experiences were beyond words. Instead, we both laughed as we watched the mighty mammals tumbling in the cold shimmering ocean.

Trixie barked.

'You're right, girl,' I said. 'We'd better get going.'

Reluctantly, we climbed back into the jeep and continued along the coast, the glorious ocean on our right. Point Clarke was located before the turnoff to the Blackwood National Park. It was one of the many tiny towns that dotted this section of the coast. Most could barely be called towns. They were motley collections of houses nestled in the hills high above the water.

A few weatherboard shacks fronted the road. Between these lay a solitary street that wound out of sight. We followed this for about five minutes as the tarred road gradually dwindled to unsealed gravel.

A stone letterbox beside a driveway indicated the entrance to Sidney Langston's property. We descended into a tiny cleft in the hill. In this, the home huddled, a modern glass and stone place reminiscent of something by Frank Lloyd Wright. Planted around it were tea trees and other native flora. It wasn't what I'd been expecting.

This is swish.

I'd expected Sidney's home to be middle-class, and this was as far from that as you could get.

Pulling up outside, Kim, Trixie, and I started across the driveway. Although the house was protected from the onshore breeze, it was still chilly in the glade. My gaze moved from the home to a walking trail that led up the side of the hill. Sidney appeared over the crest and started down.

'He looks happy,' Kim murmured. 'Not.'

'I don't think he likes visitors.'

The man reached the bottom of the trail and crossed the yard, still wearing the same scowl. As he was about to open his mouth, Trixie went bounding across and stopped in his path. Sidney glared at her momentarily as she sat there, panting. He reluctantly bent over and patted her head.

'Beagles,' he said. 'One of my favourite dogs.'

'They're great friends,' I said.

'The best.' His eyes angled up to us. 'I wasn't expecting visitors. Are you here about Vivian Shelly? The police already interviewed me about her.'

'We're just doing a follow-up. Then we'll be out of your hair.'

Although Sidney looked ready to say no, his eyes returned to Trixie, and he reluctantly nodded. 'I suppose I can spare you a few minutes,' he said.

Soon, we were inside his living room, a vast chamber with a sunken lounge and a modern gas fireplace. A painting by Australian artist Brett Whiteley decorated the wall.

Sidney's made some money over the years, I thought.

'Thanks for seeing us,' I began. 'We didn't get a chance to talk after the other night.'

'The evening didn't quite go as expected,' Sidney agreed.

'What did you think of the séance?'

He sighed. 'Not a lot,' he said. 'The whole thing was a scam.'

'Really?' No one else had spoken about it that way. 'Is there anything in particular that made you feel that way?'

'Not really. It's what I expected.'

Kim frowned. 'Then why did you go?' she asked. 'It's a lot of money to spend—'

'My wife died because of that woman,' Sidney said shortly. 'Jill always believed in that kind of rot. I never did. Not for a minute. But Jill believed. Even more so after our daughter Mia died.

'Mia had pancreatic cancer that wasn't discovered until it was too late. My wife became obsessed with contacting Mia after she died. Jill had attended a séance when she was young. It left an impression on her. She said there were things the medium couldn't have known, yet they did.' Sidney gave a bitter laugh. 'I had no intention of attending such an idiotic event. I pleaded with Jill not to waste our money. Not that I was worried about the money,' he added. 'Life was good to us. When I left school, I had an interest in medieval history. I wanted to become a history professor. My father talked me out of it. I still have an interest in history, but it was my father who talked me into following the money. I got a job with a stock-broking firm. Did well at it. Then started my own business and was able to retire early.'

His eyes grew distant. 'When Mia got cancer, we paid for the best treatment money could buy. The best *conventional* treatment, I should add. Towards the end, Jill got desperate. She wanted us to see people in India and remote hilltop villages who spruiked cancer cures. I said no. It was fraudulent and would raise Mia's hopes unnecessarily. And, by that stage, she likely wouldn't have survived the travel, anyway.' He cleared his throat. 'Anyway, I think Jill felt resentment about not try-ing those treatments after Mia died. I suppose that's why I reluctantly agreed to Jill attending Vivian's séance.'

'You didn't go?' Kim said.

Sidney shook his head. 'I refused,' he said. 'It was rubbish. And I couldn't stand some phony pretending to be our Mia. Making silly voices and spouting lies. It was insulting. But not to Jill. So she went. It wasn't an overnight stay, unlike the other evening. Jill should have been home by ten o'clock. I waited up as ten became eleven and then midnight. I was about to ring the police when they turned up on my doorstep.' His eyes grew moist. 'They said Jill had veered off the road. Possibly to avoid hitting an animal. The car rolled, and she was killed.'

He got up, walked stiffly to the window, and stared at the

stunted trees. He turned to us. 'You want to know why I went the other night?' he asked. 'I wanted to see the con that Jill had been exposed to. I went there knowing the entire event was a farce. I intended to sue both Vivian Shelly and Tony Hall. In fact, I still intend to sue Tony. I'm almost...' he struggled for the word '...*regretful* that Vivian is dead. Death is too good for those types of people. They should be flayed alive.'

I fixed my gaze on him. 'Sidney,' I said. 'Tony and Vivian were receiving threatening messages for some time. I suppose they were from you?'

'I'm sure a lot of people hated them.' The man swallowed hard. 'Now I think I've answered enough questions. I'll ask you to leave. I need some peace.'

15

Doris glanced up from the desk as I entered the Gazette's front office.

'You've had some calls,' she said.

'Why do I have to be so popular?'

'Just lucky, my dear.'

It was Monday morning. After visiting Sidney Langston the previous day, I'd gone home to help Nan knit outfits for the Zonta club. She had quite a collection, and the handover to the hospital would be a good article for the paper.

Jay was working on some reports from the local sports clubs. It was football season, and our local team—The Seagulls—was playing every weekend. Jason Kirby, their centre half-forward, had broken his ankle and would be out of action for the rest of the season.

'I'm leading with that.' Jay glanced up from his computer. 'Sound good to you?'

'Great. If it bleeds, it leads. Half of Cape Carson will be in tears over Jason's ankle.'

Sitting at my desk, I listened to my messages, most of which were people getting back to me on stories I'd been chasing for weeks. The last message, however, really got my attention.

'Hello Rosie,' the woman said. 'This is Jasmine Ward. I used to be Vivian Shelly's personal assistant. I've got information you might find interesting.'

Jasmine had left her phone number and asked me to call her back. Within minutes, I'd spoken to her and had an appointment set for eleven o'clock. After hanging up, I glanced at my watch.

'Look at the time,' I said. 'It's coffee o'clock.'

I headed down the road with Trixie at my side. A bright, crisp day had risen at Cape Carson after the previous day's strong winds. Reaching Percy Street, I was so focused on the calm bay I didn't notice the person ahead of me until I walked straight into them.

'Oh my goodness!' I said.

'Rosie!' Yvonne said. 'How are you?'

Although I tried not to stare, it was hard not to. The brunette was wearing a tangerine-coloured shift dress and looked gorgeous. I tried hard not to think about my dowdy suit combination.

And this woman is staying with Todd, I thought, dismally. *What chance have I got?*

I tried to sound cheerful. 'I'm fine,' I lied. 'So sorry about running into you. I need to watch where I'm going.'

'It's hard not to look at the ocean,' Yvonne agreed. 'It's quite meditative. Are you going for a walk?'

'Grabbing a coffee.'

'Mind if I join you?'

'Of course,' I enthused, although I felt like running in the other direction. 'I usually go to Sandy's.'

'Great. That's where Todd and I went last night.'

So now he's taking other women to our diner!

My mind was going crazy, and I wasn't sure why. Todd wasn't my boyfriend. He was my friend, and I'm sure that's how he felt about me.

So why was I seeing green?

We went in, ordered coffee, and settled into a booth at the back. Now I was sitting opposite Yvonne, I could see her face clearer. She'd had some work. No doubt about that. A nip here. A tuck there. Still, she looked good for her age. Maybe she had naturally good skin.

Sandy brought out our coffees. Yvonne had ordered a black coffee, the same as Todd. I felt like a blimp ordering my jumbo double-shot caramel latte.

'So you went to school with Todd,' I said, keen to not draw attention to my bucket of coffee. 'Has he changed much?'

'Have you ever seen the Rusty Jones Mysteries?'

The kid's show had been on when I was young. Although Todd was a child star on the program, I could barely remember him or it, and I said as much.

'He was skinny back then,' Yvonne said. 'It was only as he went through high school that he put on muscle.'

'For the show?'

'Mostly to fight off the bullies.'

I frowned. 'Really?'

'He was given a hard time for being on the show. Actually, it was relentless, and not many kids stood by him. My family lived next door, so we'd known Todd and his parents for years.'

'I see.' I'd known nothing about this. It had never occurred to me that Todd would have struggled in such a way. I knew his relationship with his father was difficult; his father relentlessly pushed his career, leaving Todd with little time to enjoy his childhood. 'So you were on his side?'

'I beat up the bullies when they picked on him.'

I laughed but stopped when Yvonne didn't. 'Really?'

'Absolutely. I did Tae Kwon Do from the time I was five. Broke the nose of one kid.' Yvonne grinned. 'Gave another a double blackeye.'

'That must have been quite a sight.'

'Wish I'd taken a photo.' She sipped her coffee. 'Todd speaks well of you. Said he even showed you his trains.'

'Oh yes,' I said. 'I mean, I'm glad he says nice things. And that train set's a hoot. I've never seen anything like it.'

'Everyone needs a way to unwind.'

Yvonne asked me what I did for hobbies, and I told her about my love of movies and books. As it turned out, her favourite films were film noir movies of the forties and fifties, with her best-loved actor being Humphrey Bogart.

'He sure packed some emotion into a single expression,' she said.

I agreed. Much to my surprise, I was warming to Yvonne. Still, I was doing my best to not think about her sharing the house with Todd. Glancing at my watch, I told her I had to get moving.

'Working on a story?' she asked.

'I'm *always* working on a story.'

Grabbing my coffee, I wished her a good day and headed off. It was time to meet up with Jasmine Ward. I was soon on my way to her home on the west side of Cape Carson. It was a small timber place set back from the road, nestled amongst grevillea and bougainvillea. My knock at the front door was answered by frenzied barking.

A woman, stick skinny with brown hair and eyes, answered the door. She smiled pleasantly as a mob of unruly dachshunds barked relentlessly at her feet.

'Quiet!' she yelled. 'Or I'm sending you all to the pound!'

The dogs quietened, although I doubted her threat had

anything to do with it. The woman invited us in, and after the dogs had given Trixie a good sniffing, we followed her inside to a small sunroom at the front of the house.

Jasmine got straight to the point. 'I was Vivian's assistant for six years,' she said. 'And it was both the best and worst experience of my life.'

'In what way?'

'Vivian promised a lot and delivered little. I worked day and night. Took her from obscurity to famous the world over. You think she wrote those books?'

'She didn't?'

'Vivian *dictated* those books. Most of what she said was barely in English. I had to massage her ramblings into something readable.'

The books had been phenomenally successful. It was hard to believe that this woman in this tiny house in suburban Cape Carson had done most of the writing. Still, stranger things had happened.

'Okay,' I said slowly. 'Let's get to the nitty-gritty of things. Was Vivian the genuine thing or not?'

Jasmine nodded. 'Vivian was real,' she said. 'Absolutely.'

'So she really could speak to the dead?'

'Vivian gave me messages from my grandfather.'

'She couldn't have discovered those things herself?'

The woman hesitated. 'It's possible,' she said. 'But it would have taken a lot of research. And I saw Vivian do it with other people.'

'You're familiar with cold reading?'

Jasmine had never heard of it, so I explained what it involved. 'That may be what the phonies do,' she said resolutely. 'But not Vivian. She could really communicate with the other side.'

It was pointless arguing. 'Okay,' I said. 'So what happened with you and Vivian? Why did you leave?'

'I didn't leave. I was fired. Tony came along, and Vivian was infatuated with him. It was love—no, obsession—at first sight. It's hardly surprising. Tony Hall's a good-looking man.'

'And Tony? He felt the same?'

Jasmine snorted. 'I doubt it,' she said. 'Tony was flat broke when they first met. Apparently, he'd put a lot of money into some investment scheme, and the whole thing went bust.'

'You know he was dating Melissa Martin?' I said. 'They'd been together for years?'

Picking up one of her dachshunds, Jasmine stroked its back as she spoke. 'I know,' she said. 'Melissa was dumped faster than a hot potato. She didn't deserve that. The woman came to the house one day after Tony dumped her and made a scene. Eventually, she left, but I came close to calling the police.'

'That's terrible.'

'Poor Melissa was treated like a pariah. I bumped into her in town one day, and she was in a terrible state.'

I thought back to how Melissa was the night of the séance. 'She was at the séance the other evening,' I said. 'Her mother had recently passed.'

'I knew she'd been unwell. To make matters worse, I heard her father's suffering from early-onset dementia. I did see Melissa again, though, and she was doing better. I think she'd come to terms with the whole breakup.' Jasmine shook her head. 'She was more forgiving than me. I might have killed Vivian myself.'

'A few people didn't like Vivian,' I said. 'If you don't mind me asking, where were you on Wednesday night?'

Jasmine snorted. 'At home with the gang,' she said, patting her dog. 'And before you ask, I don't have any witnesses.' She frowned. 'But I thought it was an open and shut case. A burglar killed Vivian?'

'I'm just following up on a few leads.'

'That burglar story sounds like a load of rubbish to me. It wouldn't surprise me if Tony didn't hire him to kill her.'

I asked if she'd ever heard of Zane Bennett, but she hadn't. After a few more questions, I thanked Jasmine and headed to my car. The gaggle of dogs continued to bark unceasingly from inside the house as I climbed behind the wheel.

'Thank goodness you're quiet,' I told Trixie.

She panted happily, and I gave her a doggy snack. I sat quietly and thought about everyone I'd spoken to. I'd interviewed all the séance attendees, but hadn't spoken to anyone who knew Zane. All I knew was that he was a mortgage broker with a gambling problem.

I sat in my jeep for a few minutes with my phone, searching the internet for a mention of him online. Eventually, I came across an old story. He'd been involved in an assault where a man had ended up in hospital. His sister—Terri Bennett —had blamed the whole incident on the victim.

After finding her on social media, and sending a message, I returned to the office. As I settled back at my desk, my phone buzzed, and I saw that I'd received a response.

Thanks for making contact.

My brother Zane is innocent—I'm sure of it!

16

'Now that's what I call a gaggle of kids,' I said.

'I think a gaggle is a group of geese,' Kim replied.

'So what do they call a lot of kids?'

'Expensive.'

We'd just knocked at the front door of Terri Bennet's home. At least six children, all skinny with blonde hair, were running around the front yard. She lived in Needleworth, a biggish town north of Cape Carson.

The town's ice cream company had been running successfully for the last century and employed at least a quarter of the town population.

Terri's house was two streets back from the heart of town. I could see why the kids were playing outside. The racket was so deafening I wouldn't want them inside either.

'They might not all be hers,' Kim pointed out.

'I don't know.' I looked more closely. 'They all look the same.'

At that moment, the front door flew open, and a woman who looked identical to the kids appeared. 'Keep the noise down, you lot!' she yelled, then turned to us. 'Rosie?'

'And Kim and Trixie,' I said, introducing them. 'You must be Terri.'

She invited us inside, telling the kids again to stay quiet. We followed her into a lounge room that was scattered with toys. The noise of the kids outside was almost matched by the racket of a peach-faced parrot squawking in a corner cage.

'*Shhh!*' she told the bird.

It obediently fell to silence.

Terri offered us cups of tea, and we were soon sipping from these as we sat around a coffee table. I could immediately see the similarity between Terri and her brother.

'Thanks for coming,' she said. 'It's important that people know the truth about Zane. He didn't commit that murder. He couldn't have.'

I remembered the body lying in the chapel.

'How can you be so sure?' I asked.

'Zane was making money. He didn't need to rob anyone.'

'Were you close to your brother?'

The woman shook her head. 'Not for a long time,' she said. 'Zane went off the rails when he was a teenager. Hung out with the wrong crowd. That's how he got that teardrop tattoo under his eyes. Me and mum and dad hardly had anything to do with him for years.'

'Then what happened?'

'He came good. Got his certificate as a fitter and turner. Did that for a few years. Then he met someone who worked at a mortgage broking firm. Zane wanted a change, so he got a job as a mortgage broker.'

'There's a lot of numbers in finance,' Kim said.

'Zane was fine with numbers. He was a bright guy. Like I say, he hung with a bad crowd at school and went the wrong way.' She hesitated. 'And there was the gambling.'

'So he had an addiction?'

Terri nodded. 'It was a real shame,' she said. 'As soon as he made money, he spent it. He was lucky, though. I'll give him that. Never ended up in serious debt.'

'Was he making a lot of money?' I asked. 'In mortgage broking, I mean.'

'It takes a long time to build. Brokers make their money from an upfront bonus and trail commissions. He was making deals regularly, though. His future looked bright.' Her eyes glistened with tears. 'That's why Zane killing that woman makes no sense.'

'The police think it was a robbery gone wrong.'

'Still makes no sense.'

Kim interjected. 'You mentioned not being in contact with Zane much.'

'That was because of how he was years ago. We had a huge argument and didn't speak. Then he contacted me a while back. Wanted to reconnect.'

'Did he ever mention Vivian Shelly and Tony Hall?' I asked.

'No.'

There was something, though, in what Terri was saying. It had struck me as odd from the beginning: Zane's appearance. He had worn black, but his style was smart casual: jacket, t-shirt and jeans. He looked ready to go out for the evening. Not rob someone's home.

'You need to look at Tony and Vivian,' Terri insisted. 'Snoop around their home. See why Zane was really there.'

I exchanged glances with Kim. There was no mistaking the alarm in her eyes. She was never comfortable with me doing anything illegal.

Neither was I, although my definition of illegal was more flexible than hers.

'Have you been to Zane's place?' I asked. 'Since he passed?'

'No. I don't have a key, although I know I'll have to clear it out.' Her eyes filled with tears. 'Please help me. I know Zane is innocent.'

I promised to do what I could. Thanking Terri for her time, we said goodbye and headed back to my jeep. The kids were still running crazily around the house.

'So,' I said to Kim. 'Do you think Zane was on the straight

and narrow?'

'I don't know, but I'm sure of one thing.' Her mouth was set into a thin line. 'The last thing we're doing is breaking into anyone's house.'

'As if I'd do something like that!'

'You've broken into more homes than a locksmith!'

'I have not!'

'You have! Every time we go somewhere, you want to break into their house!'

'I do not!'

'You do!'

'You know,' I said, thoughtfully, 'now that you mention it, taking a look around the Lake House would be helpful—'

Kim yelled. 'That's the same as breaking in!' she shrieked. 'It's trespassing! Trespassing! T-R-E-S—'

'Kim,' I soothed. 'You don't have to spell trespassing. I know how it's spelled. We'll go to the front gate and see if Tony Hall answers. That's all.'

'You're fibbing again, Rosie.'

'No, I'm not. I'll push on the buzzer and see what happens.'

Kim glared. 'All right. Just as long as you don't break in! It's dangerous. D-A-N-G—'

'I know, I know, Kim. Dangerous and illegal. Received and understood.'

We drove across the open countryside, taking arterial roads

through kilometres of Australian bush until we arrived at the front gates of Vivian Shelly's property. I thought about the first time I'd been here. It was barely a week ago, and so much had happened since then.

'Now what?' Kim asked.

'Rather than buzz at the gate, I can ring Tony to ask if we can see him.'

Kim stared at me. 'O-kay,' she said uncertainly. 'But what if he's not home.'

'Then we'll deal with that.'

I rang Tony and told him I'd like to ask a few more questions about Vivian and what would happen with her latest book. He said he wasn't home, but we could get together some time over the next few days.

'Well,' I said, hanging up. 'That settles that. Tony's not home. I suppose, while we're here, it won't hurt to take a little look around the outside.'

Kim's mouth dropped open. 'Rosie Ryan!' she said. 'You're the most insufferable person that I've ever met! You told me—'

'I'm just looking around the outside. You can stay in the car.'

I took out my phone and examined the area using Google maps. I could enter using the same path Zane had used to access the chapel.

I drove around to it, aware that Kim was quietly fuming. If I wasn't careful, she'd explode at any moment.

After a few minutes, I pulled into a small glade at the side of the road where a rough trail led through the undergrowth.

'Excellent,' I said. 'I'll just take a little look.'

Kim said nothing.

'Are you annoyed with me?' I asked.

'What do you think?'

'I promise—absolutely and completely promise—that I will not break into the house. I'll take a walk around the outside. That's all. You have my word.'

As I left the jeep, Kim got out the other side. 'I can hardly let you wander about alone,' she grumbled. 'Anything could happen.'

Sometimes no reply was the best reply. Leaving Trixie in the car, I put the window down and started up the trail. This must have been the way Zane Bennett came. The path was not often used, but people had been through here recently.

The police must have trampled through here after Vivian's murder, I thought.

'Zane must have left his car in the same glade,' I said. 'I should ask Todd if it revealed any clues.' We continued along the overgrown path. 'Zane must have carried a torch. You couldn't get through without one.'

'There was no torch near his body. Maybe he used the light on his phone.'

'That's possible.' We continued along the trail. 'Hey, look

where we are.'

We'd reached the rear of the ancient stone chapel. The back door was closed. I tried it experimentally, but it was locked. The thin trail rounded the building and under some trees to emerge onto the lawn. Beyond lay the path around the lake and the house beyond.

'Zane watched Vivian enter the chapel,' Kim said thoughtfully. 'He waited until she was finished and then forced his way in. They struggled and were both killed.'

'That's the official story.'

'You don't believe it?'

Something was nagging at my senses, and I wasn't sure what. I eyed the house. Tony had said he wasn't home. There was no movement at the building. 'I'm taking a closer look,' I whispered. 'You wait here.'

Kim groaned. 'Don't be silly,' she said. 'I'm coming with you. If we get caught by Tony, I'm telling him you're a mad woman, and I'm trying to stop you.'

'You think he'll believe that?'

Kim's jaw dropped. '*Seriously*?' she said. 'You *are* a mad woman! I *am* trying to stop you!'

I had no good reply to that. We stepped from the dense shrubbery, scurried across to the path, and crept around the edge of the lake. We were in clear view of the building. If Tony were lying and was inside the house, he would spot us.

Let's hope he was telling the truth.

We reached the rear of the building. Some curtains were pulled open, and we could see inside. The place looked empty. No sign of Tony or any servants. He and Vivian had said they only intermittently hired help. Kim and I trailed along the side of the house, stopping near the window that was Vivian and Tony's bedroom.

'That's odd,' I said, pointing to the ledge beneath the glass. 'One of the ornaments is gone.'

Kim stared. 'You're right,' she said. 'The one with big ears.'

'A ceramic fish.'

I couldn't think of a single good reason why it would be gone. Tony couldn't have taken an instant dislike to it.

After all, the thing had probably been sitting on the ledge for months. Maybe even years.

Where is it?

We continued around the house, peering into bedrooms as we went. Thankfully, no one was around. Tony had been telling the truth. Explaining our presence wouldn't be easy. We continued past the Scarlet room. From this angle, in the cold light of day, the room bore none of its spooky qualities. It looked like a boardroom that an amateur interior designer had painted the wrong colour.

Arriving back at the location of the missing fish, we rounded the lake to the chapel. Just in time, too, as we heard a vehicle approaching, down the driveway. We started back along the path but had only taken a few steps when Kim grabbed my arm and pointed into the bushes.

'Look,' she whispered. 'Are they flowers?'

'They are,' I said, stepping into the undergrowth. 'Or were.'

What had been a bunch of long-stemmed red roses, wrapped in delicate pink tissue paper, and wrapped with a red ribbon, had been reduced to a sodden wilting mess by the week of torrential rain. The wrapping paper was falling apart, but it was still possible to make out the sticker that had held it together.

'*Dell's*,' I said, reading the label. The flower shop owner was Rita Dell, the sister of Graham Dell, who owned the garden centre. 'These are from Cape Carson.'

'What are they doing here?'

It made no sense. A bunch of roses tossed into the garden. Did Tony leave them here? Or Vivian? Or a staff member?

Zane came this way, I thought. *He must have left them here.*

But why? No one in their right mind would take a bouquet of flowers to a burglary. Kim stepped further into the dense undergrowth.

'Look,' she said.

She picked up an equally sodden white box, wrapped with a red ribbon. Pulling it open, she revealed assorted handcrafted chocolates. 'I think these are from Hogan's Sweets in town,' she said.

'So Zane brought flowers and chocolates to a robbery,' I said. 'That makes no sense at all.'

We continued back to the glade, where we'd left the car. We stowed the items in the boot of my jeep. After finding the flowers, it seemed a good idea to search for more clues. It took a few minutes, but we eventually found a fresh cigarette butt under a tree.

'Dunhill,' I read the filter.

'Did Zane smoke?' Kim asked.

I quickly made a call to Terri. Hanging up, I turned to Kim. 'No,' I said. 'He was a non-smoker. And some good news, too. I've got Zane's address. We can go over there to check out his place.'

17

An hour later, Kim and I were outside a block of villas in Palmdale, a small inland town about twenty kilometres down the coast. Palmdale sat in a narrow valley surrounded by acres of bush. Besides a petrol station—a must out here—the main street was comprised of a butcher, a general store and farm machinery warehouse.

'Rosie,' Kim said in that voice that I knew all too well. 'How exactly are we getting into Zane's house?'

'We've got Terri's permission.'

'Um. Yeah. But that doesn't answer my—'

I got out of the jeep and started down the driveway.

There were a dozen detached villas. Zane's place was almost at the end, which was for the best because we needed some privacy. Especially if we were almost-kind of-really breaking in. The homes were like tiny doll's houses. It was strange to think of Zane the burglar cum killer living in one of these places.

I inspected the address Terri had given me. 'Number Nine,'

I said. 'This is it.'

The lawn on each side of the doorstep was green, but only because it was Astroturf. The red geraniums lining the wall under the two front windows were an improvement.

'Rosie,' Kim said firmly. 'How are we getting in?'

'Terry gave me permission—'

'You said that before—'

Before she could continue, I went to the front door and shoved. Locked. Of course. Remarkably few people kept their doors unlocked these days. Especially when there were killers running around.

Or investigative reporters.

The fences on each side of the building were white picket, though short and easily scalable, which was fortunate because that was what I needed to do. I'd gotten one leg over when I spotted movement from the corner of my eye.

'Excuse me?' the woman said, peering over the side fence. 'What are you doing?'

I stared at her. 'Real estate,' I said, forcing a smile. 'I'm with the real estate agency. We're handling the sale of this...er, lovely home.'

'Really?' The woman was elderly with ringlets of grey hair and a heavily lined face. 'Zane's selling?'

I told the woman that Zane was unfortunately deceased.

'My goodness!' she said. 'What happened? A heart attack?'

I thought of the knife jammed into his chest. 'Something like that,' I said. 'Anyway, we're just taking a look around.'

'Can I get a card?'

'Card?'

'A business card. My kids are insisting I sell up.'

I reached blindly into my handbag, not sure what to do. Then I spied something and pulled it out.

'Here you go,' I said, handing over the business card.

The woman glanced at the picture on it. 'Cape Real Estate,' she read. 'And you're Amanda?'

'That's me.'

Fortunately, being a supportive mother, I always carried a supply of my daughter's business cards for interested parties.

'You don't look like your photo,' the woman ventured.

'Oh.' I laughed nervously. My daughter looked lovely in the picture. And all of her twenty-three years. 'I've aged,' I shrugged. 'Divorce.'

She examined the picture again. 'It shows.'

Kim scaled the fence after me, and we scooted around the back before more real estate opportunities arose. A few steps led to the back door. The windows on each side were firmly locked, so we continued to the other side.

'That bathroom window's open,' I said, peering up. 'But only a few inches. There's no way I could fit through.'

I stared at Kim.

She stared back.

'What?' she said. 'It's not bad enough that you've lied to a nice old lady? That you've impersonated your daughter? That you've trespassed on someone else's land? Must I be part of your latest crime spree?'

I liked that phrase *must I be*. It sounded Shakespearean, and I decided to use it more often. 'Yes,' I said patiently. 'We have Terri's permission to be here. She practically told me to go inside and search, so that's what we're doing. Now you need only to squeeze in through the window. It'll be easy.'

Grumbling, Kim allowed me to give her a leg up. It was a tight fit, but she soon let me in the back door.

'I don't know how you talk me into these things,' she said.

'I have strange hypnotic powers,' I said.

We made our way methodically from room to room, starting with Zane's bedroom, then the living room, bathroom, and kitchen. The place was tidy for a bachelor pad. I'd be sorely disappointed if I'd expected to find piles of stolen goods lying about. The place looked like a typical bachelor's home. He had some half-eaten pizza in the fridge and a video game console in the living room. Zane had been sharing the bedroom with a bench press and a set of dumbbells.

Zane hadn't been a big reader, although, to his credit, the few books he owned were all about self-help and improving your life. There were no copies of *How to be a Better Burglar* or *How to Get Away with Murder*.

We finished searching the kitchen from top to bottom. 'Nothing,' I said. 'And we don't have Zane's phone, so we can't check his call history.'

'What will we do?'

'Hmm. We haven't checked the most unpleasant place of all.'

'If it's the toilet, you're on your own.'

'Almost as bad: the rubbish bin.'

The kitchen tidy was half-full of food scraps and junk mail. There were also packets of protein bar wrappers. And then—

'Ah-ha,' I said. 'Receipts.'

'Anything helpful?'

'Groceries, mostly.' I examined them. 'Although there's one for the flowers and another for chocolates and a restaurant.'

'Let me guess: the flowers are from Dell's Florist?'

I nodded. The chocolates were from Hogan's sweets, just down the road from the florist. The restaurant was further afield: the Rubicon, in Hamilton, a regional town two hours west of Cape Carson.

'Hamilton's a long way to go for a meal,' Kim mused. 'I wonder who he was seeing.'

'Are you okay with a drive?'

'I suppose. Just as long as we don't have to break in any-where.'

'I can't make any promises.'

Shaking her head, Kim followed me to the car. Half an hour later, we were in Dell's florist, where I showed the receipt and a photo of Zane Bennett to Rita Dell. She was the spitting image of her brother with a broad face and friendly eyes.

'Oh sure,' she said, examining the receipt and the photo. 'These came from us. And I remember this fella. He was in here on Wednesday.'

That was the day of the murder.

'Did he say who the flowers were for?' Kim asked.

'No. Although he said something about the woman being out of his league.'

'Really?' I said. 'Out of his league?'

Kim and I thanked her and scooted up to the sweet shop. This was run by Marlene Hogan, the jolly woman from the Cape Carson Mystery Book Club.

Unlike Rita, Marlene shook her head sadly as she looked at the receipt. 'I'm sorry, girls,' she said. 'We make lots of sales here every day. Remembering one purchase is impossible.'

'And the guy?' I asked, describing Zane.

She shook her head again. 'No. I don't remember him.'

Kim and I headed out to the footpath. A seagull was trying to extract a food scrap from a street bin, and Trixie barked, driving it away. I glanced at my watch. Although it was late in the day, I still wanted to visit the Rubicon, though it meant we might be late for Olga's class.

'It's okay,' Kim said. 'Let's go to Hamilton.'

'Really? And Olga's class?'

'I'm not really enjoying it.'

'Really? But you're the star pupil.'

We climbed into my jeep, where Kim continued. 'I thought it would be fun,' she said, settling back as I started the engine. 'I always liked art at school.'

'I'm sorry about that,' I said. 'Olga's too arrogant for my liking.'

'It's a shame she's not more likeable, as she was one of Australia's most celebrated artists. I wonder why she dropped out of sight.'

We followed Donovan Road north out of town, driving through the bush surrounding Cape Carson and into open countryside. The word *likeable* ran through my mind as I remembered Todd's friend, Yvonne.

She was likeable and sharing the same house as him. And they'd been friends for a lifetime. Although it was hard to imagine Todd ever being a skinny kid, I knew that bodybuilders sometimes got big because they'd been bullied as kids. Todd's upbringing, I knew, had been less than ideal. His father had been somewhat of a bully, pushing Todd and his acting career. There was a fine line between encouraging a kid and shoving them with full force.

I tried not to think of them alone in his house. Anything could go on. A candlelit dinner could lead to drinks, laughter, some flirting...and then what? They didn't even need to find a hotel! The guest bedroom was only five feet away!

'Rosie,' Kim said. 'Are you okay?'

'Sure. I'm fine. Why do you ask?'

'Well, you just missed our turn, and you're gripping the steering wheel so hard, it's like you're trying to wrench it off.'

I cursed and relaxed my grip. 'Oh dear,' I muttered, pulling the car around and turning onto the right road. 'Sorry about that. I was thinking about Todd and Yvonne.'

'I thought you said she was nice.'

'She is—and that's the problem!'

Kim sighed. 'You can't expect Todd to hang around waiting for you.'

'Waiting for me? I've been waiting for him!'

'Sometimes, you need to take the bull by the horns.'

'I don't even know what that means,' I grumbled.

We continued onto Hamilton, finally pulling into the town at around three o'clock. I found the restaurant easily. The Rubicon was in what had once been an old-style Federation brick cottage at the end of a backstreet.

Some of the interior lights were on. A woman, presumably the manager, was at the front counter on the phone. I'd been concerned about getting information, but she was surprisingly forthcoming as she examined the picture of Zane Bennett.

'Yes, I remember him,' she said. 'It's the tattoo. I've never liked those facial tattoos. Mind you, he was friendly enough.'

I asked if she could find the booking for the night they had dinner. After checking their computer system, she shook her head. 'No,' she said. 'His name's Zane Bennett? Maybe he booked under a different name. Or the woman did.'

'Woman?' I said. 'So he had dinner with a woman?'

'Yes, I don't remember her too well. We had a big booking for a birthday party that night. All I recall is that the woman was attractive with long black hair.'

I exchanged glances with Kim. 'Do you have any bookings under the name Vivian?'

The owner checked the system. 'Yes, actually. Vivian Smith.'

'But the payment was through Zane's credit card.'

'That's not unusual. The person who does the booking isn't necessarily the person who pays.'

We thanked her and returned to the street.

'Vivian Smith,' Kim said thoughtfully as we got into my jeep. 'Surely that's not—'

'Vivian *Shelly*? Attractive with black hair? It sounds like her, but why were they meeting out here? And for dinner? I can only think of one reason.'

Kim's face was grim. 'They were having an affair,' she said. 'Which puts a completely different complexion on their deaths. It could have been a lover's spat that turned violent.'

'That explains the flowers and chocolate in the undergrowth, too. And Zane's appearance: neat casual.'

'It seems strange that Vivian risked having Zane at the house. Maybe he surprised her after the séance.'

'It had to be something like that, although it doesn't explain him carrying the weapons.'

'Maybe he always carried them.'

We started back for Cape Carson. There were still things that didn't make sense. Were robbery and murder always Zane's intention?

Or did a chain of events spiral out of control? And those weapons. They put an ominous spin on the whole event. Todd had said Zane owed money to the wrong people. Maybe he carried the weapons for protection.

I swallowed hard.

Terri fervently believed in her brother. She was certain he'd turned his life around. An affair between him and Vivian was bad enough without evidence proving him to be the killer. I kept my eyes on the road. It wasn't night, but the sun was low on the horizon. A bank of white and charcoal clouds sat in the distance, unleashing showers on a faraway hill.

Something niggled at the edge of my senses. Something that didn't fit.

The fish.

That's right: the ceramic fish. How did it fit into all this?

'Rosie,' Kim said, caution in her voice. 'I don't want you to worry unnecessarily, but—'

'Is it my driving? You know my driving's sloppy when I'm tired.'

'No.' Kim leaned forward to peer into the passenger side mirror. 'It's the car behind us.'

I glanced in my rear view mirror. A late-model grey Toyota with a battered number plate was about a hundred metres back.

'What about it?' I asked.

'I'm sure that car was behind us all the way to Hamilton,' she said. 'Now it's behind us again. We're being followed.'

18

'Are you sure?' I asked.

'No—but don't do anything weird. Just drive normally.'

I *was* driving normally. Of course, the weird thing about being told to act normal is that you immediately start behaving differently! 'Okay,' I agreed. 'I won't do donuts on the road or balance the car on two wheels.'

We were still over an hour from Cape Carson. I could ring Todd and ask him for an escort, but we could be mistaken about being followed. Glancing in the mirror again, I glimpsed what appeared to be a stout-looking man with glasses. He didn't look like a hit man, although the best killers probably seemed quite inconspicuous.

'I've got a plan,' I said. 'But it could be dangerous.'

'What is it?'

After dropping her at home, I could linger until she got her car. Then she could trail after me and the man to see if he followed me. Kim immediately agreed. 'I can do that,' she said. 'I've always wanted to tail a suspect. Although if he spots me, I'm not keen on chasing him at high speed. I don't like speeding. I'm a librarian.'

'Is driving at high speed against the librarian's pledge?'

'We don't have a pledge, but it's actually a good idea. We could take an oath against censorship and dogearing of books. Then we could—'

'Kim,' I interrupted, not keen to spawn a secret librarian's cult. 'Don't chase him at high speed. Don't run him off the road. Just follow him. That's all.'

We reached Cape Carson, where I dropped Kim off at her place. The man who'd been following us was good at his job. He pulled over near the corner. I waited until Kim disappeared inside, pretending to linger over my phone. Then I took off and headed across town, eventually stopping in my driveway.

Trixie and I went inside. Nan wasn't home. Probably for the best. I didn't want her worrying. I peeped out the window. There was no sign of either Kim's car or the other vehicle.

I rang Kim. 'Where are you?' I whispered although it was unnecessary. 'I'm in the house.'

'I'm following the man. He's back on Percy Street.' She paused for a moment. 'Hang on. He's heading up into town.' The next few minutes passed slowly as she updated me. 'Okay,' she said, finally. 'He's pulling into a hotel. It's the Cozy Inn.'

The place was a white timber building that had once been

a grand home. It had been transformed into a small boarding house. The lady who ran it was a silver-haired woman named Lois Dawson. Her family had lived in the area for generations. I'd written a story about her and the building when it was heritage listed by the council.

Another minute passed. 'Okay,' Kim finally said. 'He's staying there. The man's gone into one of the rooms.'

'Great.' I said. 'Don't go anywhere.'

Grabbing Trixie, we raced to the car and drove through town to the tiny hotel. I pulled in behind Kim, and we met on the footpath, our breath forming clouds in the cool evening air.

'What now?' she asked.

'Now we confront him.'

'What if he's violent?'

'Then we scream and run. Maybe not in that order.'

Kim produced keys from her handbag. 'I have keys,' she said. 'I can gouge his eyes out.'

'Surely that would be against the librarian's pledge?'

Kim pouted. 'You're no fun.'

The parking lot outside the hotel was quiet and still. We went up the front steps and into the foyer, where Mrs Dawson sat at her desk. She was knitting while watching television, her Welsh corgi, Mallowan, at her feet.

'Rosie!' she said. 'This is a pleasant surprise. What brings you here?'

I explained we wanted to talk to one of her guests. After describing the man, she told us his name was Gerald Lime, and he was staying in room Six. Kim and I crept down the hall. Various sounds came from the rooms: someone talking on their phone, canned laughter from a television, classical music.

Knocking firmly on room Six's door, I stood back and waited, my arms crossed. It was only a few seconds before the door opened, revealing a heavy-set man in a safari suit and blue-and-white striped shirt.

He frowned. 'Yes?'

'Why have you been following us?' I demanded.

The man's eyes narrowed. 'I don't know what you mean.'

'Don't lie. I'm friends with the local sergeant. I can have the cops here in minutes.'

'And I'm a librarian!' Kim added.

The man glumly motioned us inside. 'Come in,' he said. 'We can't talk out here.'

Kim and I reluctantly entered. It was a cramped square chamber with a single suitcase open on a chest of drawers. The television was playing with the sound turned down. A laptop sat on the bed.

He reached into his pocket, produced a card and I read it.

'Gerald Lime Investigations?' I said.

'You're a private eye?' Kim said.

I glanced at her. Kim had gone from fearful adventurer to starry-eyed fan girl in less than a second. This was probably the first private investigator she'd ever met. Actually, it was probably a first for me too.

'What are you investigating?' I asked. 'And why are you following me? And who are you working for?'

Gerald leaned against the chest of drawers. 'Last question first,' he said. 'I'm not at liberty to reveal my client's identity. As for what I'm investigating, it's Vivian Shelly. Or it was until she was murdered. Judging by your travels over the last few days, you've been investigating her too. That's why our paths have crossed.'

I glanced back down at the card. 'You're working for Sidney Langston,' I said. 'He paid you to investigate Vivian.'

To Gerald's credit, he concealed his surprise well, but not well enough. His eyes narrowed slightly, and I knew I'd hit pay dirt.

I continued. 'Sidney blamed Vivian for the death of his wife. He wanted you to dig up dirt on whether Vivian was real or fake. You were there the night Vivian got murdered.'

'You got evidence for any of that?' His laugh was hollow. 'Or you're just stabbing in the dark?'

'Stabbing in the dark? Not at all. You rang Sidney while we were at his house. When he answered, he called you Gerry.

That's a shortened form of Gerald. And in the street behind the property, there was a Dunhill-branded cigarette butt.' I motioned to a pack on the table. 'That's your brand.'

Kim spoke up. 'So what did you see?' she asked. 'The night Vivian was murdered.'

Gerry seemed to reach a decision. 'You're good,' he said. 'Both of you. A regular Holmes and Watson.' He sighed. 'I didn't see a lot. Just enough to confirm what the police already know. Zane murdered Vivian Shelly.'

'You saw it happen?' I asked.

'I saw Zane head up the trail. It was dark, but I saw him waiting at the rear of the chapel. Then someone appeared at the back door and waved him in.'

'It was Vivian Shelly?'

'Who else could it be? Everyone else was in the séance.'

'What about Tony?' Kim asked. 'Have you been investigating him too?'

'Tony was obviously part of Vivian's scam,' Gerry said. 'But how much of a part he played is hard to say.'

'You keep saying it was a scam,' I said. 'I'm not arguing with you, but I wonder what proof you have.'

Gerry chuckled. 'I'm naturally suspicious,' he said. 'If you told me it was daytime, I'd stick my head out the window to check. You can't contact the dead. It's hard enough getting through to an operator at Telstra. All Vivian did was cold-read her clients. Or she and Tony stalked their clients over the net. You can find a lot—and I mean a lot—about people via the net. You can also do credit and other checks if you're prepared to spend a few dollars. With the money Tony and Vivian were making, it would have been more than worth their while.

'Vivian told them what they wanted to hear. Mostly, she did no harm. She gave people hope and provided some comfort about their loved ones. Some people were probably dragged out of terrible depression and unhappiness from what she said.' Gerry swallowed. 'My own daughter passed away a few years back. You don't think I wouldn't want to talk to her? To know that she's okay?'

I thought about Frank Ryan, my grandfather. Yes, I could understand someone wanting that connection.

'But the truth matters,' Gerry continued firmly. 'The truth is important. Stealing from people is wrong. Lying is wrong. The repercussions of one of Vivian's séances could be devastating.'

He couldn't mention Sidney by name, but he may as well have. Sidney's wife was dead because she attended Vivian's séance. Vivian couldn't be directly blamed. Jill Langston's car crash was bad luck. But if she hadn't attended the séance that night...

'After you saw Zane enter the chapel?' I asked. 'Did you hear the gunshots?'

Gerry hesitated. 'Only one,' he said. 'But I know the walls of that place are a foot thick. I'm lucky I heard anything at all. Anyway, I hot-tailed it out of there. Guns and I don't mix.' He glanced at his watch. 'Now, if you don't mind, I've had a long day.'

I glanced at his card again. 'We might need to mention your name to the police.'

The investigator looked pained. 'Try to keep me out of it,' he said. 'I really didn't see anything. Just some figures in the dark.'

'I've got two questions,' Kim said.

Gerry nodded. 'Okay.'

'Will you stop following us?'

'Yes. My work is done, and I've got other jobs backing up.' He paused. 'And your second question?'

'How do I become a private investigator? It seems *really* cool.'

Gerry groaned. 'It's cool as long as you don't mind trailing cheating ex-husbands and wives,' he said. 'And photographing people to confirm insurance fraud.' He glanced at his watch again and opened the door. 'Good evening, ladies.'

There seemed no point in arguing with him. We wished him a goodnight and filed out into the street. It was dark now, and the night was cold.

'It doesn't sound like Gerald Lime had anything to do with

Vivian and Zane's deaths,' I said.

Kim nodded. 'We're back to Zane again,' she said. 'He brought flowers and chocolates. They had a lover's spat, he attacked her, and they both died.' Kim checked her watch. 'Guess what? If we hurry, we can catch the rest of Olga's class.'

'Do we have to?'

'Come on,' she urged. 'We're almost at the end.'

I reluctantly agreed, and a few minutes later, we were both pulling up outside the community centre. We got out of our cars and went inside. The art room was in darkness, and Olga was trudging up the hall, art supplies crammed under her arms.

'Ah-ha,' she said unhappily. 'I have some students.'

'Olga,' Kim said. 'What's going on? What about the class?'

'I'm sorry. The class is cancelled. No one has turned up.' She nodded to Kim. 'Even my star student is late.'

'I'm sorry,' Kim said, reddening.

'It's all right.' Her gaze fixed on me. 'You heard about the books about me at the art gallery? Stolen and burned in a bin! A crime! Will your newspaper be reporting on that?'

I studied her face. 'The Gazette reports the news as we see fit,' I said evenly. 'Maybe I can interview you sometime? Get your side of things?'

'Of course.' Olga took a card from her bag and pushed it into my hand. 'Ring me, and we will speak.'

We headed out into the night. Olga trudged away to her car, a battered old mini. It started with a cough, and she roared off into the darkness.

'So that's the end of art classes,' Kim said.

'Doesn't look like I'll be the next Van Gogh anytime soon.'

Trixie barked.

19

Todd glared at me. 'When you say you found these receipts in Zane's rubbish,' he said, 'you mean the bin was out on the street. You're not saying you broke into his home? Right?'

It was early the next day, and I'd dropped into Todd's office at the Cape Carson Police Station to bring him up to date. 'Of course,' I said smoothly. 'I'm not saying that at all.' And I wasn't saying that. Technically, I hadn't actually *said* it. Maybe I had gone into Zane's home, but that was with his sister's permission. 'The important thing is that we now know Vivian was having a fling with Zane.'

Todd examined the receipts. 'And this man Gerald Lime?' he said. 'The investigator? He saw Zane on the night of Vivian's death?'

I explained that Gerald had seen someone letting Zane into the chapel and it had to be Vivian. Everyone else was at the séance.

'All right,' Todd said thoughtfully. 'I'll contact Gerald.' He frowned at me again. 'This puts a different light on things. Zane seems to have been having an affair with Vivian, but everything went wrong. An argument. A lover's quarrel. And they both ended up dead.'

I pursed my lips. 'His sister Terri thinks Zane was on the straight and narrow.'

'I know. I've spoken to Terri. I can understand her wanting to think the best of her brother. We all want to think well of our family members. But it doesn't get much clearer than this.'

I got up to leave. 'Oh, I bumped into Yvonne yesterday.'

'So she said.'

'Everything's going well?'

'Yes.' He levelled his gaze at me. 'Why do you ask?'

'Just wondering.' I said I'd better get moving. 'I'll let you know if I find out anything.'

'Please do. It's actually a law that you bring evidence to the attention of police.'

'Really? Did you invent that yourself?'

'No. It's the Magna Carta or something. One of those big official documents.'

I returned to the street with Trixie at my heel. Dropping to one knee, I gave her a doggy snack as I rubbed her chin. I felt upset. The thought of Todd and Yvonne together created a big lump in my throat, and I wanted to burst into tears.

Don't be ridiculous! I told myself. *He's a grown man! He can do whatever he wants with whoever he wants!*

Sure, another part of my brain said. *But I want him to do it with me!*

My eyes were moist as I walked down to Percy Street and turned toward the diner.

'Rosie!'

I turned. 'Duncan,' I said. He'd obviously been for a swim, and his t-shirt clung tightly to his body. He pushed back his red hair. 'Been for a dip?'

He looked closer at me. 'Are you okay?'

'Something in my eye. I'm grabbing a coffee. Feel like joining me?'

He said he could do a takeaway but had to keep moving. He needed to be home for an online meeting. As we headed into the diner, I asked about his audition.

'It went well,' he said, smiling. 'That's actually what the call's about. They want to see me in person.'

'Fantastic. So you could be the next Hamlet?'

'One of many.'

Sandy, behind the counter, handed us our coffees.

'Look, Rosie,' he said. 'I'd better get moving. I don't want to be late.'

Saying goodbye, he bounded down the steps and out of sight. I glanced over at Sandy, who was shaking her head.

'What?' I said.

'You're amazing, girl!' she said. 'A new hot guy every time I see you!'

'Just a talent, I guess.'

I forced a smile and headed back out to the street where I'd left Trixie. The day had dawned bright, and the air was crisp, and it left me wondering why I was feeling so miserable.

It's Todd, I thought.

In the back of my mind, I'd always thought our relationship was going somewhere. Slowly, admittedly. Some might even describe it as glacial.

Still, I thought we were heading in the same direction. One day he'd stop being a cop, and we'd become an item.

And now—Yvonne.

The worst part of it was that she was so *nice*. Couldn't she be awful so I could hate her? That would make things so much easier. I glanced along the beach path and saw Kim jogging in my direction. Giving her a wave, she raced over to me.

'Hey you,' she said. 'You've got a funny look on your face. Any particular reason?'

I told her about meeting with Duncan and my feelings about Todd and Yvonne. She rolled her eyes. 'So you don't even know if they're dating?' she said. 'You know you could just ask?'

'That sounds really intrusive.'

'You're a journalist. Asking questions is part of your job.'

'True.' I wasn't sure what to do. It was hard to casually bring it into the conversation. *Are you dating your flatmate? Are you really just old friends? Or is there more to it?* I changed the subject. 'I'm heading back to Zane's home.'

'Right,' Kim scowled. 'So you're just driving past to look, aren't you? You're not actually breaking in.'

'It's not breaking in when—'

'Rosie!'

'I'll be fine,' I said airily. 'You busy today?'

'Only work. They're beginning to think I'm doing the job by correspondence.' She gave my arm a brief squeeze. 'Please be careful.'

I promised I would and headed to the car with Trixie. We were soon stopping outside Zane's home in Palmdale. The villas surrounding his house were quiet. It looked like everyone had gone out for the day. I went to the rear and felt more than a bit of trepidation as I peered up at the bathroom window.

Last time, I was here with Kim. *Skinny* Kim. *Small* Kim. *Petite* Kim. For me, struggling through the bathroom window would be like pushing a sausage through a keyhole.

Trixie whined.

'What is it, girl?' I asked, ruffling her neck. 'Everything's okay.'

A sound came from the back of the house. I went around to the door. It was open a crack, and I was sure we'd closed it behind us. Mounting the steps, I cautiously pushed the door open and peered inside. Everything looked unchanged. I listened hard. Nothing.

I headed into the kitchen and glanced in the bin before moving onto the living room. All the while, I had the oddest feeling that someone else had been here recently. I inhaled. What's that smell? Perfume? Or a men's aftershave?

Maybe someone's been here.

I started down the hallway—and then everything happened at once. Trixie broke into a flurry of frenzied barks as a figure stepped from a room, a person in a puffer jacket, jeans, and a balaclava. I froze in terror as their eyes narrowed on me. All of Kim's warnings came back in a flash.

Don't break into people's homes...it's dangerous...against the law...anything can happen...

I tried to think of something to say. To do. Some brave act that would get me out of trouble. In a movie, the hero would break into a series of karate moves. Unfortunately, as a kid, I'd had to choose between karate and cricket, and cricket won out. I would have been fine if I'd brought a cricket bat.

So I screamed.

As weapons go, it was pathetic but produced a result. The person charged, slammed into me, and kept going as I went flying. The back of my head struck the floor, and I lay senseless, staring up at the ceiling. Fluffy clouds gathered before my eyes, and I had a terrible sinking feeling.

Do not pass out, I thought. *Stay conscious!*

Shaking my head, I rolled over as Trixie licked my face.

'I'm okay, girl.' I struggled to my feet and staggered to the back door. The man—if it was a man—was gone. I went out the front and peered up and down the street. Trixie whined again. 'We're fine. I promise.'

I wasn't sure if I was saying it for her benefit or mine. There was only one thing I could do, and it was something I didn't relish. I rang Todd and told him what had happened. Half an hour later, he arrived with a siren blazing and wearing a worried expression.

'Rosie, are you all right? Do you need an ambulance? Are you injured—'

'I'm fine,' I assured him. 'Just a few bumps and bruises.'

'In that case—'

'Please don't lecture me.'

'I wasn't going to.' His face softened. 'I'm just glad that you're okay.'

As I stared into his eyes, my heart gave a little flutter, and I felt simultaneously like bursting into tears and jumping for joy. There was no mistaking the look Todd was giving me. He wasn't looking at me; he was looking *into* me.

'Are you dating Yvonne?' I blurted.

'Huh?' He stared at me. 'What?'

I mentally kicked myself. 'I mean,' I continued. 'I was just wondering. That's all...I'm a journalist...asking questions...'

A faint smile played across his lips. 'How hard did you hit your head?'

'I...well...'

'Are you asking for yourself or for the paper?'

I felt myself reddening. 'Both,' I snapped. 'We're doing an article on the ten most aggravating men in Cape Carson—and you're top of the list!'

'Great,' he said, grinning. 'You know how competitive I am.'

'Oh...you!'

Todd asked me to write a written statement, and an hour later, I was back in Cape Carson. I headed to the library, where I found Kim cataloguing books at her desk. I told her what had happened.

'You crazy woman!' she said. 'I told you not to go there! Did you recognise the guy?'

'I'm not even sure it was a guy,' I confessed. 'It all happened so fast. It could have been an average-sized guy or a bigger woman. He was wearing a balaclava, so all I saw were his eyes.'

'You wouldn't recognise his eyes?'

I groaned. 'Kim,' I said. 'He—or she—had two of them. I have no idea as to their colour. One of them could have been glass for all I know.'

'Do you think?'

'You idiot!' I punched her arm. 'I don't know how—'

My phone rang, and I glanced at the screen: Edwina Parkridge.

'Rosie,' she said after I answered. 'I was wondering if you could come over for a chat. There's something I need to speak to you about.'

'What is it?'

She hesitated. 'I'd rather talk to you in person,' she said. 'It's something that doesn't make sense. I've been trying to work it out since the night of the séance.'

'Okay,' I said uncertainly.

What's this about?

'Bring your friend Kim if you like,' Edwina continued. 'And can you print the photo you took of Vivian and me?'

'Of course.'

We set a time for six o'clock. Hanging up, I told Kim I had to go to the office and I'd pick her up when I finished. She made me promise not to break in anywhere between now and then, to which I muttered *I'll try not to.*

Back at the office, Jay was out doing an interview with the President of the local Lions Club.

I checked my emails and scanned the usual messages from people with tips about stories. A few looked promising, although several wouldn't even make it into a small paper like the Gazette.

...I have a recipe for pizza topping that my husband says is the best he's ever had...

...see lights out at sea at night. I'm sure they're UFOs...

...build totems that look like famous people. My latest looks like Albert Einstein...

I stared at the last email. Almost as if the universe came into perfect alignment, Harry's voice came from his office.

'Rosie?' he called. 'Have you rung Charlie Holmes about his totems yet?'

'Not yet! But gosh, I'm looking forward to it! Hold the front page because—'

'Is that sarcasm I detect?'

'Not at all.'

A moment passed.

'Is that more sarcasm?' Harry yelled.

'Yes. No. I'll ring him now.'

Picking up the phone, I soon had an enthusiastic Charlie Holmes on the line. 'They're works of art,' he said proudly. 'Although most people don't appreciate them as I do.'

I remembered what Harry had said about pictures in the paper. And he was right. Photos of Charlie's totems could make for an interesting human interest story. Charlie could see me immediately, so I was soon on my way to his home on the west side.

Once I arrived, I was more than a little surprised that I hadn't heard about Charlie and his passion before. At a glance, his yard looked like someone had grown a forest of trees, only to cut them down to head height, leaving only the trunks. On closer inspection, however, I realised these were the totems: dozens of brightly carved and painted monuments. They filled the front yard and trailed all the way down both sides of the building.

Among the crowd, I spotted the famous Australian bushranger, Ned Kelly, a few former prime ministers, and a couple of movie stars, John Wayne and someone who looked disturbingly like Darth Vader.

This wouldn't have been so bad, except they all faced onto the street. There was something eerie about them all staring at me. Even Trixie gave a concerned whine as we got out of my jeep.

'I know how you feel,' I muttered. 'It's like arriving at Easter Island.'

The sound of banging echoed from the rear of the property. Charlie was hard at work on another piece, and I wondered how the neighbours felt about the ongoing racket. As if to answer this question, a woman emerged from her house across the road and arrowed over.

'Are you from the council?' she asked.

'No. The newspaper.'

She introduced herself as Carla Clark. 'Well, thank goodness you're here,' she said. 'Something's got to be done.'

'About the totems?'

'They're ghastly,' Carla said, shuddering. 'Some of us think they're haunted.'

I laughed. 'Really? They're not that bad.'

'You don't think?'

I gazed back at the yard of misshapen faces. Maybe they wouldn't have been so awful if they weren't staring at me. And there were so many of them. I felt completely outnumbered. 'Well,' I amended. 'They're an acquired taste.'

Carla grimaced. 'Yeah,' she said. 'Like weed killer.' She said she'd already complained to the council on multiple occasions. 'The whole neighbourhood's up in arms about them. That man had better watch himself, or he'll be sorry!'

Upon saying this, she marched off down the street.

'Well,' I said to Trixie. 'Not everyone's a fan.'

We headed up the front path and had barely knocked on the door when a stocky balding man wearing a carpenter's apron flung it open.

'Rosie Ryan!' he said. 'I saw Carla speaking to you! Interfering old cow!'

I assumed that last line was about Carla and not me. 'She didn't sound pleased about your, er, art works.'

'She's a menace! I'm creating art to make the world a better place. That terrible old biddy wouldn't know great art if it fell on her!'

Glancing back at the sea of figures, it would have been easy for that to happen. 'Can you tell me how you build your totems, Charlie?' I asked. 'Are they made from old telegraph poles?'

'They are, indeed.'

He stepped outside and I followed him around the house to the rear. Back here was jammed full of even more totems than the front yard.

'Goodness,' I muttered.

Charlie showed me his carpentry workshop.

It was a sophisticated setup with a workbench, sanders, planes and even a band saw. He explained that a totem usually took him a week and sometimes two to build. I took notes as he spoke.

A monitor was lodged into the roof in the corner. The screen showed the front yard. 'You watch your front yard?' I said. 'Have people tried to steal your totems?'

He glanced at the monitor. 'That's a recording from last week,' he said. 'Someone left a nasty note under my front door. I'm checking to see who it was.'

'Not everyone appreciates your art?'

'There are always critics,' he said, darkly. 'And look at all the timber I'm recycling. It could all go into landfill, but now it has a second life.'

'What do your customers think?' I asked, scribbling.

'Customers?'

'Yes, the ones who buy your totems.' I stopped writing. 'Or do you give them away?'

'Oh no,' he said, shaking his head. 'They're not going any-where.'

'Sorry?'

Charlie patted his work-in-progress on the head. It could have either been Freddie Mercury or Errol Flynn. It was hard to tell. 'No,' he said. 'Others wouldn't appreciate them as I do. They're staying right here.'

'They're staying...'

Seeing how the front and back yards were almost filled, I wondered what he'd do once he ran out of room. I forced a laugh. 'I suppose you can always store them inside,' I said.

Charlie shook his head. 'There's no room inside,' he said. 'It's full.'

'Of...?'

'Totems.'

Not for the first time, I wondered what had happened to my promising journalistic career. I'd interviewed some of the biggest names in Hollywood and dozens of local stars. Now I was speaking to a man with a fetish for building totems. I wondered if he had plans for global domination, but somehow

I managed not to ask.

'Exactly how many totems have you made?' I queried.

He stroked his chin. 'About two hundred,' he said. 'You can't get into the bedroom anymore. The whole cast of *The Lion King* is in there.'

'I'm sure. And you're not selling your totems because—' I glanced at my notes '—others wouldn't appreciate them as you do.'

'That's about right.'

Sighing, I snapped a few pictures before thanking Charlie and escaping back to my jeep. The sea of faces watched me grimly from the front lawn as I rang Harry.

'Good grief,' he said after I filled him in. 'Seems Charlie's a bit obsessive?'

'Only if you can call building a timber army to take over the world obsessive.'

'But you got some pictures?'

I stared back at the wooden faces, and they stared back at me. 'Yep,' I said, more than a little unnerved. 'I got pictures.'

20

Kim came bounding out of the library. 'You're late,' she said. 'I thought you'd forgotten about me.'

'Sorry.' I explained that I'd been held up writing the story about Charlie and his totems. 'It was hard to choose an angle: *Local Artist at Work* or *Out of Control Obsessive Draws Ire of Neighbours.*'

'What did you decide on?

'*Local Artist Draws Ire of Neighbours*. It gives both sides of the story.'

We drove across town to Edwina's place. It was getting dark, and the storm that had threatened earlier had not eventuated. No lights were on in Edwina's home. I knocked at the front door, and we waited.

'She mustn't be here,' Kim said after a while.

'That's odd. Edwina said to turn up at six.'

I knocked again before trying the front door and finding it locked.

'I hope she's okay,' I said. 'Maybe we should—'

'We are not breaking in!' Kim said firmly. 'I don't care if her house is on fire and she's stuck under her fridge! We are not entering her home!'

'All right,' I soothed. 'Relax. I wasn't going to suggest we break in. Just that we check around the back.'

'No.'

I rolled my eyes. Kim could be awfully stubborn sometimes. 'Come on,' I said. 'It will only take a minute.'

Groaning, Kim followed me. 'You know I'm a librarian? Right?' she said. 'My life is supposed to be about books, the joy of reading, and ensuring people have access to accurate information? It's not supposed to be about trespassing or breaking and entering?'

'Maybe it should be added to the job description.'

We skirted around the house. As we reached the backyard, I spotted a figure at the bottom of the stairs.

'Edwina!' I cried.

We raced over, but the woman was cold and motionless. Kim checked her pulse. 'Oh no,' she said. 'She's dead.'

The back door was open, and a cat sat perched on the top step. My mind returned to what Edwina had said.

I love my cats though they do get underfoot.

'Could she have tripped over a cat?' I asked.

'Maybe.'

Blood was on the stairs and there was a big gash on the back of Edwina's head. It looked like she'd stumbled over a cat and turned sideways as she fell down the stairs. I rang Todd and gave him the bad news as Kim examined the blood pattern.

After dealing with Todd's ribbing—you've found *another* dead body—I got off the phone to see Kim frowning at the body.

'Rosie.' She pointed to drops of blood on the wall. 'Look at that blood spray. I don't think it matches someone falling down the stairs.'

I peered at the spray. 'You could be right,' I said. 'We'll see what Todd and the cops say when they get here.'

The distant sound of sirens filled the air. Soon, vehicles were skidding to a stop outside the house, and cops were swarming the location. After checking on the body, they went behind the house, leaving Kim and me to wait out the front. We climbed into my jeep as the evening grew colder. Half an hour passed before Todd appeared, a grim expression on his face. I wound down the driver's side window.

'What do you think?' I asked.

'Well,' he said soberly, 'it *looks* like she fell down the stairs with a cat being the likely culprit. I counted at least fourteen felines, and I suspect there's more hiding.'

Kim spoke up. 'Todd,' she said. 'I'm no expert at blood splatter analysis, but that pattern on the wall could be someone being struck. Maybe from behind.'

'Maybe you should leave it up to the experts,' Todd said kindly.

'There are books on criminology in the library. I've read every single one.'

Todd bit his lip. 'I've got a forensics team on the way,' he said. 'We'll see what they say. Meanwhile, I'm curious as to what brought you ladies here. You had an appointment with Edwina?'

I explained that she'd asked us to visit, requesting that I print the picture I'd taken of her on the night of the séance. Todd asked to see it.

'Doesn't seem special,' he said, examining the image. 'No offense, Rosie, but it's not a great picture.'

'I agree.'

'Did other people take pictures on the night?'

'I don't think so. People wanted to remain anonymous.'

'And Edwina didn't say what she wanted to talk to you about?'

I shook my head. 'No,' I said. 'But there was something wrong from the beginning. Even during the séance, she had an odd look on her face. I wondered if she doubted Vivian's ability.'

'Except,' Kim said, 'we asked her later how she felt about the séance, and she was fine.'

'So what changed?' Todd asked.

'I don't know. It would be quite a blow to Edwina's ego if she decided that Vivian was a fraud. Edwina believed in her completely. Even owned all her books.'

'And she'd met Vivian before,' I pointed out. 'Edwina was a long-time fan.'

The forensics van pulled up behind my jeep. Todd asked us to head to the station with him and fill in a statement. We agreed, and it was an hour later when Kim and I finally emerged into the night.

We were both exhausted—and hungry.

'I'm starving,' Kim said. 'A quick visit to Sandy's?'

'You've talked me into it.'

We drove there and were soon nestled into a booth. As our meals arrived, my ex-husband, George entered.

'Oh dear,' I said.

His eyes narrowed on us. George looked ready to walk back out again, but then he sauntered over. 'Kim,' he said. 'Rosie.'

His expression when he looked at me was like he'd stepped into something smelly and sticky. I ignored it. 'Getting some food?' I asked.

'Just some takeaway.' For a moment, he looked ready to say more. 'I'll see you both later.'

George grabbed his takeaway and disappeared into the night.

'Well,' Kim said. 'That could have been worse.'

It could have been better, too.

I didn't want to argue with George.

Besides sharing a daughter, we also lived in the same town. What had happened regarding his brother was regrettable, but we had to get through it.

Kim and I ate in silence. She looked tired, and I knew I was exhausted. So much had happened, and we had a lot to process. I couldn't get the image of Edwina Parkridge out of my mind. The sight of her at the bottom of the stairs. Her cats. The blood.

Why did Edwina want to see us? What did she want to talk about?

And what was so important about that photo?

I took the picture out again and examined it. The image showed Vivian and Edwina side by side. Vivian's expression was like a movie star on the red carpet, but Edwina looked like a child who'd been handed a candy jar. *There's nothing special about this picture.* Maybe it was something else about the night. My mind went round and round as I remembered everyone at the séance: Vivian, Tony, Sidney, Tania, Alicia, Russell, Melissa and Edwina.

Kim snored.

She'd fallen asleep clutching a half-eaten burger!

'Kim,' I said.

'Huh? What?'

'Come on. I'll take you home. We both need rest.'

Half an hour later, after dropping Kim at home, I was stumbling back in the door of my place with Trixie at my heels.

Nan was watching the television. 'Big day?' she asked.

'Enormous.' I told her about finding Edwina dead. 'The woman wanted to speak to us about something, but I have no idea what.'

'You look dog-tired, Rosie,' she said. 'Have you thought about sticking to traditional journalism? Doing stories about flower shows and surf carnivals?'

'I do those stories. But then we have all these murders.'

'We haven't had a murder at a flower show yet. Or a surf carnival.'

'Not yet,' I said, yawning. 'But there's still time.'

21

I awoke early to find the rain lashing my window and the sky overcast. Everything was soaked, and the streets were wet with rivulets of water running across in broad sweeps. It looked like it had been raining most of the night. I shivered as Trixie yawned and joined me at the window.

'It's a grey day,' I told her. 'A good day to stay in bed.'

And that would have been a fantastic option, except I had work to do. Whenever I was stuck, I found that going for a walk helped clear my mind. And I was stuck now. Vivian Shelly's murder still didn't ring true and Edwina's death was far too soon to be a coincidence. I wondered what Kim was doing, so I sent her a text message.

She rang me seconds later. 'Hey Rosie!' she said, sounding entirely too bright. 'What's up?'

'I'm looking out at the weather. It's very wet.' I listened and heard falling rain. 'Where are you?'

'Up on Millicent Drive.'

'You're running? In the rain?'

'It's invigorating.'

'So is jumping out of a plane without a parachute. Feel like a coffee?'

'Sure.'

I told her I'd meet her at Sandy's. Leaving Trixie at home, I made my way up the road, dressed in a puffer jacket, rain boots, and jeans. The drizzle had momentarily stopped, although there was plenty more on the way.

At the end of my street, I took the track through the thick scrub towards the coast. Big drops of water tumbled down from overhanging trees. A bird gave a disconsolate cry.

The ground was muddy as I trudged towards Cut Rock Lookout. Finally, the track opened up onto the car park and the cliff beyond. Great voluminous waves heaved and pushed against the coast. Surfers were making the most of it on the east side of the lookout. A little rain made no difference to them.

Surges of water came crashing into the cut in the rock, sending light spray bursting up through the top. I lingered at the railing, peering down into the abyss where a maelstrom of foam and deep water frothed in a murky mix. I gazed out to sea, looking for whales. At first, I saw only the rippling cobalt blue waves tinged by white cotton tips. Then a colossal bulk broke the surface, a mottled mixture of raven black and mottled white that thrust upwards as if searching for the sky before crashing into the heaving ocean.

I grinned. It was worth the cold and the wet to see this.

Rain fell again, great curtains of it as I reluctantly turned from the railing and plodded down the path into town. Boats rose and fell in the rippling bay as I reached Percy Street. I angled across the road to Sandy's and was soon settled into one of the window seats.

'You right there, Rosie?' Sandy asked. 'Need a towel?'

I was dripping wet. 'Do you have one?'

She returned seconds later with a towel. As I dried my hair, Sandy and I watched the rain until Kim's white Ford Focus zoomed to a stop out the front, and she came racing in.

'It's really coming down out there,' Kim said and then took a closer look at me. 'You go swimming?'

'Feels that way.'

After returning Sandy's towel, we ordered coffee. Kim and I perched together at the front, watching the rain belting down. I'd always enjoyed watching the rain. There was something strangely hypnotic about it.

My phone beeped: Harry.

Got a minute to chat?

I rang him back. 'Hey Harry,' I said. 'What's up?'

'Morning, Rosie,' he said. 'I had a tipoff from one of the nurses at the hospital. Olga Farago has been admitted.'

'Really? What happened to her?'

'I'm not sure. Can you drop by?'

'Sure.' Fortunately, I had my coffee in hand, and the caffeine was kicking in. 'I'll go there now.'

Kim offered to drive us, and we were soon marching in through the front entrance of Cape Carson Public Hospital. A nurse at the front desk pointed us down a corridor, and we bustled into Olga's room. The artist was perched on the side of her bed, a bandage on her forehead. She wore her oversized clothing and high-heeled shoes. Her shawl lay in a heap beside her.

'Kim!' Olga cried. 'And Rosie! You have come to see me! Bad news travels fast!'

'What happened?' I asked.

'I was walking on the beach when a man approached me. He asked if I was the artist known as The Spider. When I said *yes*, he took out a small hammer, like one you would use to break rocks, and he hit me across the head. Then he ran away.'

'You were on the beach? What beach?'

'On the sand below the lighthouse.'

'Did you ring the police?' Kim asked.

Olga shook her head. 'I did not want to trouble them,' she said. 'It all happened so quickly, and I could not identify the man, anyway.'

'Goodness,' I said coolly. 'You're lucky you weren't seriously hurt.'

'I know. You should put something in the paper about it. This constant persecution of me is unforgivable. Maybe an article—'

'I don't think so.'

'But people should know about my attack—'

'There was no attack,' I said flatly. 'Any injury you have is self-inflicted. And you're also responsible for stealing the books from the Art Centre library and burning them.'

Olga's mouth turned downward. 'You should not say such terrible things,' she said. 'I am The Spider. I was a finalist in the Archibald, I won the Garibaldi International art prize, the Toff-Selenzky Prize, the—'

'You're a liar,' I said and turned to Kim, who was staring wide-eyed at me. 'I'm sorry. She's been lying to us the whole time.'

'How do you know?' she asked.

'Only Robert Li and I knew what had happened to her books.' I turned on Olga. 'Yet somehow you knew they'd been burnt in a bin. Who told you?'

Olga was flustered. 'I don't know,' she said. 'I'm sure some-one—'

'No one told you. And you fit the description of the person who stole the books from the art centre.'

'No! They were disguised—' Olga stopped. 'I mean—'

'How would you know they were disguised?' I snapped.

'And now you've just told us you were assaulted on the beach? Did anyone see the assault?'

'Well, no—'

'And do you really expect us to believe that you were traipsing around the beach in those shoes? There's not a grain of sand on them. Or your pants. You're a liar, Olga, and I'm sick of hearing your lies.' I didn't like liars, and that's one reason I was so angry. But it was more than that. This woman had demeaned everyone in her class. 'My next stop is the police station. You can explain yourself to us or the cops. It's up to you.'

Olga's chin wavered. 'I...' she turned to Kim. 'Please—'

'The truth,' Kim ordered. 'Or else.'

A tear rolled down Olga's face. 'The truth?' she said weakly. 'The truth is that I'm a fraud. I'm nothing. Twenty years ago, I was the rising star of the art scene. My installations were everywhere. On television. The covers of art magazines.' She swallowed hard as her eyes dropped. 'But then everything changed. People stopped paying for my installations, so I did more and more outrageous things to get attention. None of it worked, so I had to get a job. Me! The Spider! And you know what I ended up doing? I became a cleaner! Can you imagine it? A cleaner!'

'It's an honest job,' I said, evenly.

'But I was no longer an artist! I couldn't tell my friends I was cleaning offices at night! That I was vacuuming under desks and wiping down benches! How could I? So I dropped out. Left everyone behind. Vanished.' She stopped. 'And that's how I've lived for the last twenty years.'

'Olga,' Kim said. 'People know art's a tough way to make a living.'

'That may be true,' Olga said. 'But it's hard to face people when you're no longer at the top. You are shoved aside, and someone else takes that position.' She swallowed. 'Recently, my mother died, and I inherited her estate. I thought I could start again from scratch. That's what brought me to Cape Carson. I decided to teach art classes. But when hardly anyone turned up, and people dropped out after each class—'

'Olga,' I interrupted. 'They dropped out because of your obnoxious attitude.' I pointed to the cut on her forehead. 'And lying is no way to get publicity for yourself or your work.'

'I'm sorry. I should not have done it.'

I was still annoyed, but at least now I could understand her reasoning. 'Life isn't about fame and fortune,' I said. 'It isn't about what you can get. It's about what you can give.' I nodded to the window. 'Cape Carson's a community. We stick together. You can be part of this community, and you can make a name for yourself, but you've got to do it honestly. You've got to do it by contributing.'

'What do you mean?'

I thought. 'You've noticed the water tower at the back of town?' I said.

Olga nodded. 'The water tower is ugly,' she said. 'An eyesore.'

'Then a mural painted on it by one of Australia's greatest artists will brighten it up,' I said. 'Silos and water towers all over Australia have been decorated by artists with imagery of local people, flora, and fauna. They've become part of the tourist trail.' I fixed my gaze on her. 'Approach the council for permission. The answer will probably be yes.'

The woman considered my words. 'All right,' she said finally. 'I tried my way, and it did not work. I will do as you suggest. I will ask if I can paint them.'

'And if you do, the Gazette will write stories about your good work. I promise.' I glanced at my watch. 'Come on, Kim. We need to get going.'

We headed out of there, and Kim was soon dropping me back at my place. After getting ready, I headed into work where I found Harry in his office.

'Hey Rosie,' he said. 'Any luck with Olga Farago?'

I shook my head. 'There's no story,' I said and told him Olga was going to seek permission to paint the old water tower. 'It'll brighten up the place.'

'What a brilliant idea,' Harry said. 'Well, I suppose that's what an artistic brain gets you.'

I smiled. 'I suppose so.'

'How's it going with the investigation into Edwina's death?'

'Just about to give Todd a call.'

Harry asked me to keep him posted. I headed out to my office. Jay wasn't in yet. I settled down at my desk and rubbed my eyes as I thought about Olga. It was clear something was fishy from the moment she mentioned her books being burnt. The icing on the cake had been the lack of sand on her shoes. I'd walked along that beach a thousand times, and it took days to get all the sand off my shoes. I hoped my suggestion would pay dividends.

I rang Todd and asked him about Edwina.

'Kim was right,' he confirmed. 'She was murdered. Struck with a blunt object.'

'From behind?' I asked. 'So she knew her attacker?'

'Possibly. And we found something interesting on her desk: an article about Sidney Langston's company.'

'Really? What was it about?'

'Apparently, he sold it for a motza. Twenty million. And then it only took the new owner a few years to run it into the ground.'

'You're kidding.'

'I wish I were. Twenty million to bankruptcy in five years. That's no joke.'

'Any fingerprints on the paper?'

'None.'

I scratched the nape of my neck. 'Todd,' I said. 'Do you mind if I take a look around her house?'

He sighed. 'Rosie,' he said. 'Yes, I do mind, but I know what you're like. *Everyone* knows what you're like. You'll do it anyway, and I'll get annoyed, but then you'll turn up some clue everyone else missed. So then I'll be grateful and not throw you in the slammer where you belong.'

I was silent for a long time. 'Yep,' I said, finally. 'That's what will happen. So when will I meet you there?'

22

An hour later, the cats were scattering out of the way as Todd and I entered Edwina Parkridge's home. The neon signs had been turned off and the curtains closed. It was terribly quiet without Edwina.

'She must have been quite a character,' Todd said, gazing about the gloom. 'At least she's with her family now.'

'All Edwina wanted to do was speak to her sister,' I said. 'Now she can do that.'

We went from room to room in silence.

I hadn't seen Edwina's bedroom before, but it doubled as her office. It contained a desk, computer, and another bookshelf full of volumes about the afterlife.

Another extinguished neon sign faced her bed. It read *Laugh! There's nothing to fear!*

I felt a pang of sadness. I'd miss Edwina. Although she'd been eccentric, she was one of these people who took the party with her. Someone else would eventually move in here, discard the ornaments and signage and lighting, and her place would become just another suburban house.

Todd pointed to the desk. 'The article was sitting here. It looks like Edwina was investigating Sidney. Did she and Sidney speak on the night of the séance?'

'Not that I remember,' I said thoughtfully. 'I wonder why Edwina was looking at the sale of Sidney's company?'

'You know the strangest part of it? The printer's not even working. Judging by the dust, it's been broken for some time.'

'That must be why she wanted me to print the picture I took of her and Vivian at the Lake House.' I still had the image on my phone, so I examined it again. 'There's nothing special about this and yet Edwina was insistent that I bring over a copy.'

'You couldn't just email it to her?'

'I could, but she really wanted to speak to us.' I frowned. 'Edwina's computer is still on. Can we check her email?'

Todd agreed. He also insisted I put on gloves, making me feel like a fully-fledged detective.

If Kim could see me now!

I scanned Edwina's email. Most of the messages were about religions and psychic organisations. Edwina had also liked baking and jewellery. She had completed a jewellery design course at the local community college.

'When did she ring you?' Todd asked.

I checked my phone. 'Just after one o'clock.'

'Could she have received an email that inspired her to call?'

I skimmed through the emails again. 'The link to the séance recording was emailed to Edwina at midday.' I explained to Todd that attendees could pay for a link to the event to rewatch at their leisure. 'The email could have been the reason for her call.'

Clicking on the link, the recording began. It was eerie seeing Vivian again as she stared up into the camera.

'Tony. Can you hear me?'

'I can.'

'I welcome you all to this session. To those in the Scarlet room, I remind you to stay seated at all times during the séance. It's dangerous to break the connection once made.'

'What a bunch of baloney,' Todd muttered.

'It was frightening at the time.'

'Really?'

I considered. 'Maybe not,' I admitted. 'Imagination is a powerful thing, especially where emotions are concerned.'

We continued to watch the recording. Todd snorted a few times as Vivian assumed other people's identities. By the end of it, I was beginning to feel foolish myself. My phone rang: Harry.

'Where are you?' he asked.

I told him.

'Can you drive over to Charlie's place? There's some kind of protest happening.'

A protest? Over his totems?

'Sure,' I said and hung up. I told Todd I had to get moving but asked if I could forward the séance email to myself. 'I might spot something that we've missed.'

'Like a ghost lurking in the background?'

'You never know! Stranger things have happened!'

'No problem. Just let me know if you see anything. You might need help if the killer happens to be,' he made a ghostly *woooooooo* sound, 'from the other side.'

I rolled my eyes. 'I'll be in touch.'

A few minutes later, I was pulling up outside Charlie's place. While I wouldn't call it a protest, it would be fair to describe the half a dozen neighbours as a picket line.

They were parading past his home with signs that read *Keep our Street Safe* and *Scariest House in Town.*

'Good grief,' I muttered. 'People *really* don't like these totems.'

Carla Clark arrowed over as Trixie, and I got out of the car. 'Rosie!' she said. 'I'm glad the media's here! We're fed up with this crazy man and his ugly statues!'

A few more neighbours wandered over to have their say. One woman claimed the statues frightened her children. Another said he thought they were possessed. Someone else declared their eyes watched as she passed. I got some quotes before asking Carla if she'd approached Charlie about the totems.

'I've tried speaking to him,' she said. 'He says things that aren't fit for publication.'

I asked her to accompany me while I spoke to Charlie. Soon, the three of us were grouped around his kitchen table with The Beatles, Rolling Stones and Abraham Lincoln peering over our shoulders.

'What you people don't understand,' Charlie said, 'is basic property ownership. That's my property out there. My land. I can put my totems out there till the cows come home.'

'They'd never come home!' Carla snapped. 'It's too scary out there!'

'Is a compromise possible?' I suggested. 'Some middle ground that satisfies everyone?'

'I don't see how,' Charlie said. 'Making my totems is the only thing that keeps me happy.'

There was something in the way he said it that made me pause. 'When did you start making them?' I asked.

'Last year. Just after my wife, Pari, died. It keeps me busy.'

I glanced around the room. 'And you never sell them?'

'Do you really think people would buy them?'

Carla pounced on this. 'Certainly!' she cried. 'People are always looking for homemade items at the monthly markets.'

'But I've got no way to transport them.'

'Charlie,' Carla said. 'I've got my trailer. I can take them down. You could fit about twenty in the trailer at a time.'

The man slowly nodded. 'Okay,' he said. 'They are taking up some room. People may be interested. And it would give me something to do.'

'I'd buy one,' I offered. A single totem in the corner of the yard could be quite appealing. 'At the right price.'

'All right,' Charlie said. 'I'll try it.' He fixed his gaze on Carla. 'I can't have you people stealing them. You kidnapped Winston Churchill last night! I know you took him.'

Carla grumbled. 'Yes,' she said. 'Winston Churchill is in my garage.'

'You can have him for fifty dollars.'

'Fifty dollars it is.'

The two shook hands. I told Charlie we'd run a story about him selling his totems at the local markets in the next Gazette. Carla headed off as Charlie worked out which ones he'd take.

'So it was definitely Carla who stole the totem?' I asked.

'Sure was. Caught her on my video camera.' He chuckled. 'Come and take a look.'

I followed him to the workshop, where he opened a file on his computer. The image was quite clear, showing Carla creeping into his yard, grabbing Winston Churchill, and dragging him away.

'She could have just had him,' Charlie said, smiling. 'I can make another.'

One of the other monitors showed the front yard. 'Looks like everyone's left,' I said.

'Oh, that's footage from last week. Someone else nicked Katy Perry and Bob Hope. Neighbourhood kids, I think.'

After getting a few final details from him, I returned to the jeep. Trixie settled into the seat beside me, and we took off. Something was niggling in the back of my brain. It was something I'd seen but not seen. It was right in front of my face, but I didn't understand its significance.

Reaching Percy Street, I stopped the car and wandered over to the beach. Big bulbous clouds stretched as far as the eye could see. Fingers of bright sunlight pushed through like spotlights across the ocean.

It was a beautiful sight, but I felt a sudden chill.

'No,' I muttered. 'It's not possible.'

I reached into my pocket, took out my phone, and focused on the picture of Vivian and Edwina. Staring at the image, the puzzle pieces started to come together. Slowly. One piece at a time. What I was thinking was impossible. It was too outlandish. And yet it all made sense.

Trixie cocked her head.

'You're right, girl,' I said. 'I've got it. I know what really happened to Vivian Shelly—and why!'

23

As it begins, so it ends.

All the participants of our little play were gathered in the Scarlet room. Kim looked happy enough. So did Todd and Constable Jim Turner. The two cops were guarding the door in case the guilty party should try to escape.

Vivian Shelly's previous assistant, Jasmine Ward, was here. So was Tony Hall, the man who had taken her role and eventually his place as Vivian's husband. Each looked thoughtful as if waiting to see how events would play out. Alicia and Russell Warren were here too. She looked confused, and her husband apprehensive.

Judging by the way Tania Knight was wringing her hands together, she was worried too. The skinny woman was peering out the window, her eyes fixed on the lake, a slight frown creasing her forehead. Sidney Langston sat with his arms crossed, looking like he'd rather be somewhere else—anywhere else—than back in the Scarlet Room.

Terri Bennett was here as well. It was only fitting that she should hear what was to be said about her brother. The only other occupant of the room, Melissa Martin, was listlessly scrolling through her phone as if she had somewhere better to be.

'I'd like to thank everyone for coming here today,' I said. 'It's important that you're all here, so everyone finds out what really happened to Vivian Shelly.'

A momentary silence was followed by Tony Hall clearing his throat. 'What really happened,' he repeated. 'What do you mean?'

'Vivian was killed by that burglar,' Jasmine said.

'It certainly looked that way,' I agreed, nodding. 'It seemed that Vivian finished the séance, but before she could return to the house, she was confronted by Zane Bennett. Although he'd never been in trouble with the police, we discovered he had a gambling problem.'

Terri spoke up. 'Zane was a good guy. I don't care what anyone thinks.'

'*Good guys* don't murder,' Tony said.

'Zane didn't kill anyone.'

Terri looked ready for a fight.

'We discovered a lot during this investigation,' I continued. 'Thanks to Terri, we were able to access Zane's home. We found evidence that Zane was seeing someone. We also found dead flowers and a box of chocolates behind the chapel.'

'Flowers?' Tony said, frowning. 'Chocolates? What are you saying?'

'It seems that Vivian was having an affair.'

Tony Hall's mouth fell open. 'What?' he muttered. 'That's not possible. We were happily married.'

'Yet the evidence points to it. Zane brought flowers and chocolates for a woman. He'd commented about the woman he was seeing being out of his league. There was a restaurant booking under the name of Vivian Smith. Even a sighting of a black-haired woman at the restaurant with him.'

'No...' Tony shook his head. 'No...you're mistaken...'

'When Kim and I discovered this, it put the case into a whole different light. The killing at the chapel wasn't a random attack. It was a lover's quarrel gone wrong and they were both killed—'

'No!' Terri Bennett leaped to her feet. 'That's not true! Zane wouldn't do that!'

'You're right,' I told her. 'Zane wouldn't do that.'

'What?'

'Sit down.'

She sat, and I continued. 'As I say, that's how it looked. Of course, there were a few inconsistencies. A few minor things that didn't make sense. One was the ceramic fish on the ledge outside Tony and Vivian's room. It was there the day of the séance and gone a few hours later. And why was Zane carrying a gun and a knife to a romantic rendezvous? It doesn't make sense.

'So let's consider another possibility. What if Vivian were murdered by someone else?' I turned to Jasmine. 'You were fired by Vivian when Tony came on the scene. And you knew about the rear entry into the property.'

Jasmine's mouth turned down. 'I had no reason to murder Vivian,' she said. 'I was getting on with my life.'

'I'm sure you were.' I turned to Melissa. 'Then we have you, Melissa. You and Tony were together before he met Vivian. That must have broken your heart. You must have hated both Tony and Vivian.'

Melissa's eyes met mine. 'Yes,' she said calmly. 'I did hate them. Of course, I hated them. My heart was broken. But then, as time passed, I realised the only person I was hurting was myself. I had to get on with my life. The only reason why I came here that night was to contact my mother.' Her voice caught. 'And even that didn't work.'

Tony Hall's eyes turned from Melissa to me. 'And Rosie,' he said. 'Melissa was here when Vivian was murdered. We all were.'

'Oh yes,' I said lightly. 'We were all here.' My eyes turned to the rest of the group. 'But others wanted Vivian dead too.'

'Not me!' Alicia cried out. 'And Russell told me what you

discussed about his accident. He would never harm anyone!'

'That accident was a long time ago,' Russell said, shifting uneasily. 'It's old history.'

'It takes time to heal wounds,' I said, my gaze turning to Sidney Langston. 'Of course, the greatest tragedy of all was the loss of Sidney's wife, Jill. She was driving home from a séance when she had an accident and died. Sidney even employed a private eye to investigate Vivian and Tony.'

A smile twisted Sidney's face. 'And you were astute enough to catch him. Bravo.'

'And then there was Tania,' I continued. 'The woman whose son had died.' My eyes shifted to her. 'A grieving mother might be angry—no, *enraged*—if a medium were pretending to be her son.'

'I was satisfied with Vivian's reading,' Tania said coolly.

I didn't answer her. 'In the midst of this,' I continued, 'we had the death of Edwina Parkridge. She came to the séance to communicate with her sister. At first, she seemed satisfied, but later, she looked puzzled. As if something were wrong.'

'What was she puzzled about?' Kim asked.

'I didn't know. Not for a long time. Edwina asked me to print a photo I'd taken that night. There's nothing special about it, just an ordinary photo of Edwina and Vivian.' I turned to the others. 'Then Edwina asked to see us. As it turned out, she'd rung me immediately after receiving the link to a video of the séance. She'd obviously watched it again before calling. But what was so special about the séance? We were all here when Vivian and Zane died.' My gaze swept the room. 'Or were we?'

No one spoke. Even Kim was staring at me with confusion. 'Well,' she said. 'We were all here except for Melissa. She turned up just after the séance started.'

'That's right,' I said. 'Melissa had a call from her father.'

'He has early-onset dementia,' Melissa said defensively. 'I told you that.'

'And he calls you every night? At the same time?'

'Yes. What of it?'

'Rosie,' Kim said carefully. 'Vivian was still alive when Melissa returned to the Scarlet room. And Zane. They were both killed *after* the séance ended.'

'Were they?' I let the words hang in the air. 'Are we sure of that?'

Tony gave a hollow laugh. 'Rosie,' he said. 'Have you gone crazy? We were all in the Scarlet room. We spoke to Vivian during the séance.'

'No,' I said quietly. '*You* spoke to Vivian. We watched while you spoke to her. In fact, you both instructed us not to interact with Vivian during the séance.'

'She couldn't be interrupted. Only I could act as a conduit between her and the group.'

'How convenient,' I said as I turned to the others. 'So what did we really see? Vivian left the room, rounded the lake, and then we saw her enter the chapel. Our attention turned to the video screen, and we watched Tony conduct the séance. But besides some interaction at the beginning and end, Vivian did all the talking. She talked so much that we could have been watching a recording rather than a live event.' I paused. 'In fact, that's what we were watching: *a recording*.'

I studied each of their faces, the last one being Todd. A small smile played on his lips.

Sidney was the first to speak. 'You're wrong, Rosie,' he said. 'Tony spoke to her. She spoke back—'

'Rehearsed beforehand. You remember Tony told us a few times to be quiet? You probably noticed that a control panel is beside his seat. If we got too unruly, he could cut the connection if things didn't go according to plan. As it turned out, everything went perfectly well.'

'Perfectly well?' Alicia asked. 'Why would Vivian agree to such a thing?'

'Tony has a science degree,' I said. 'I was able to contact the university and find out his speciality. It's low-frequency sound. You may not be aware, but a lot of research has been done into sound and its effect on the human nervous system. There's a frequency around nineteen hertz that's been shown to induce feelings of discomfort. You can't hear anything at that range, but you can feel it.' I nodded to the wall. 'I bet Tony and Vivian installed sound equipment behind that wall to do such a thing. It was to add some pizazz to their performance. A technology room at the end of the house controls audio, lighting, and temperature for the whole building. While the video played, Vivian was to go in there and manipulate the controls.'

Tony snapped. 'That's a lie!'

'If only that were true. Your interest in Vivian was purely for her money. You told her about the technology and convinced her that a few technical tricks would earn you even more. That's why she got rid of Jasmine. A secret shared is no longer a secret, and it was too risky letting another person in on the lie.

'Vivian believed you. But then I suppose she believed you in most things because she loved you. That part, at least, is true. She was a woman in love, and love blinds people. She had no idea she was just a pawn in your twisted plan. A plan that had been concocted by you and the woman you really loved—the woman you *always* loved—Melissa Martin.'

Melissa's gaze had been on the table. It was only now that her eyes met mine. 'Tony and I split up ages ago,' she said quietly. 'You know that.'

'No,' I said. 'You *appeared* to split up. What really happened was that you both saw how smitten Vivian was with Tony. He's a handsome man but not wealthy. Neither are you. And you could both see your future: a lifetime of struggle, of working and scrimping and saving.

'But you could shortcut the process. If Tony were married to Vivian, and if she were to die, then he would inherit her fortune—' I stopped and took a deep breath. 'And then the two of you could be together. *You could have it all.*'

Silence filled the room.

'Of course,' I continued, 'you both needed airtight alibies. What better way to make yourselves look innocent than to be with a roomful of people when she was murdered?

'Vivian suspected nothing. She entered the chapel, pressing the light switch that I assume also activated the video. While we watched the pre-recorded show, Vivian would creep back across the lawn in the dark and return to the house. In the technology room, Vivian would manipulate the gadgetry: turn down the temperature and lighting, and turn up the low-frequency sound.

'At least, that's what she thought would happen. That's what she expected. That was the plan. Instead, what happened was that Melissa entered the chapel through the back door and killed her.'

'That's idiotic,' Tony said, looking away. 'Zane Bennett murdered Vivian. From what you've said, they were having an affair. They had a quarrel—'

'No,' I said. 'Zane thought he was dating a woman who

called herself Vivian. She visited him at his office. Flirted with him. Maybe even said she was married, so their relationship had to remain secret. She was attractive. Stylish. She'd even booked dinner at an out-of-the-way restaurant under the name of Vivian Smith.' I paused. 'You know, that never really made sense. If Vivian were trying to hide her real identity, why make a reservation using the name Vivian? The only reason that makes sense is that if someone came snooping afterward, they would assume that Vivian Smith was Vivian Shelly.

'That's what Kim and I assumed. And we were wrong. None of us realised the woman Zane was dating was really Melissa Martin. She wore a black wig in case anyone enquired about her at the restaurant.' I focused on Melissa. 'I'm not sure what ruse you used to get Zane to come in the back entrance. Maybe you said your husband was going out, and it was safer if you waited in the chapel. I'm not sure. Whatever story you used, I know that Zane reached the chapel expecting to meet you there. What he didn't expect was to be murdered.

'You'd already murdered Vivian. Now you stabbed Zane and put the gun in his hand. You fired a second time to leave trace evidence of gunshot residue on him. You then hurried back to the house to join the séance. We thought your phone call had finally finished. Vivian was still on the screen speaking. No one suspected that you'd just murdered two people: Vivian, and a man she'd never met, Zane Bennett.

'The séance concluded, and I suggested we take some photos in the chapel. If I hadn't come up with the idea, Tony would have conjured up some reason to get us, or someone from the group, to accompany him: he needed someone to act as his alibi. Kim and I followed him into the chapel and found the two bodies. As far as everyone was concerned, it was a robbery gone wrong. Later, it seemed to be a lover's tiff. No matter. It was case closed.

'Later, I was attacked at Zane's house. I suspect that was you, Tony. You went there to tidy up loose ends. You didn't know that Kim and I had already found the receipts for the flowers and chocolates.'

'This whole story is ludicrous!' Tony snapped. Angry tears shone in the corner of his eyes. 'They were having an affair! This is all so much...fantasy...there's no evidence—'

'But Edwina was the one who found the most damning evidence,' I continued. 'She spotted it during the séance.'

'Spotted what?' Kim asked.

'Vivian's necklace,' I said. 'The one she wore all evening had red and blue stones. The second she reached the chapel, however, the stones on her necklace were green. Edwina couldn't understand why. She might have even thought there was some paranormal reason for it.

'That's why Edwina wanted to double-check the photo I'd taken of her and Vivian. After watching the replay, she knew something was wrong. She didn't realise that Melissa was part of the charade. I suspect Edwina mentioned it to Melissa, and that's who killed her. Zane and Vivian's murders had been planned to perfection. This time, Melissa had to act quickly. She needed to cover her tracks, and the best way to do that was to try to frame someone else.

'There was a report about the sale of Sidney's company in Edwina's office. At first, it sucked me in completely.' I glared at Melissa. 'And that's what it was supposed to do. Divert our attention. But then, a few things didn't make sense. Edwina's printer hadn't been working for some time, so when did she print it?

'And, most damning of all, why were there no fingerprints on the paper? This could only mean one thing: the article was a red herring, designed to point us in the direction of Sidney Langston.'

'Rosie,' Melissa said. 'You have no evidence of anything. Without evidence—'

'The fish.'

She stared at me. 'What?'

'The fish on the ledge outside Vivian and Tony's bedroom. It went missing the night of the séance. I always wondered what happened to it. Had Zane taken it? Had it been taken by someone earlier? It was only while I was putting all this together that I understood its importance. On the night of the séance, when you returned to the room after your call, your neck was bare; you weren't wearing your scarf.

'I'm guessing that when you murdered Vivian and Zane, you got some blood on it. You had to dispose of it quickly. But where to hide it? You couldn't risk hiding it in the chapel, the house, or the property. If the police found it, It would be game over. The ideal place was the lake, but you needed something heavy to weigh it down.' I paused. 'So you tied your scarf to the fish and tossed it into the lake.'

Melissa paled. 'No,' she said. 'No...I...'

'Police divers will scour the lake and they'll find it in minutes—'

'No!' Melissa leaped to her feet and pointed at Tony. 'He made me do it! I didn't want to kill her—'

'Shut up!' Tony yelled. 'Shut up!'

But it was too late now. There was no stopping Melissa. With her resolve gone, she was still trying to blame Tony as they were arrested. Tony, for his part, wore a helpless, sad expression. Everything they'd done, all their preparations, had resulted in failure. He turned to us just before he was frogmarched from the room.

'You know the worst part of it?' he said. 'Vivian didn't need any trickery. She really could speak to the dead. She was the real thing.'

Then they were led away. Silence settled over the room. No

one seemed to know what to say. They looked as shellshocked as I'd felt when I realised what had happened. Finally, Sidney cleared his throat. 'That's some of the most impressive deduction I've ever seen,' he said. 'I should have hired you instead of that private investigator.'

'He seems quite competent,' I told Sidney. 'But you shouldn't have sent those threatening letters. Including that email to my office.'

'I don't know what you mean.'

'Let me think.' I stroked my chin. 'What was the wording? *Fraudsters like you should be hung, drawn, and quartered.* You used a similarly antiquated expression at your home: *They should be flayed alive.* And the email message: *She was probably murdered by her scoundrel of a husband.* Most people wouldn't even think to use that kind of language.'

He'd told us he had an interest in medieval history and wanted to become a history professor. His love of it was all too obvious in his correspondence.

Still, Sidney shrugged. 'I know nothing.'

He did know, but it didn't matter. Not really. Tony and Melissa were going to jail, and that's what mattered. My eyes shifted to Tania. 'The truth is important,' I said. 'Don't you think?'

Tania stared at me. 'What do you mean?'

'And respect for people who have suffered tragedies.'

'Rosie,' Russell said. 'Tania lost her son.'

'That's right.' Tania looked ready to flee from the room. 'I lost my son and—'

'No,' I said. 'You didn't lose your son. You never *had* a son. What you had was an interest in getting a publishing deal. That's what brought you here. There was a boy named Peter Night who drowned. You found his name and created a tribute website in the name of Peter Knight with a K. If it were discovered by the real family of Peter Night, they would think it was a different child.'

'You're...no...'

'That website has existed for less than a year. Your real name is Ava Bronhurst, and you write books debunking the paranormal. Your last was about UFOs. This time you decided to go for larger bait. You created a false identity, made up the story about a non-existent son, and paid to attend the séance. You knew Tony and Vivian would run their usual con by trawling the internet for information, and you were right. You caught them hook, line and sinker.'

Ava—the woman known as Tania—scowled at me, her hands clenched into tight fists. 'We should be on the same side,' she said. 'You want the truth, and so do I.'

I regarded her coldly. 'The difference is that I don't exploit the death of a child just to clinch a publishing deal,' I said. 'Or lie to people who have lost loved ones.'

She sneered. 'You'll always be small time,' she snapped. 'A nothing journalist in a nothing town—'

Kim leaped to her feet. 'Shut up!' she snapped. 'Don't you dare say that!'

My friend looked so furious that I thought she might attack Ava. The woman fell back into her chair and didn't say another word as Kim and I marched from the room.

'Sorry I lost my cool,' Kim said as we reached my car. 'But I couldn't let her say that.'

I felt touched that Kim had come to my defence. 'Well,' I started. 'I don't—'

'Cape Carson's *not* a nothing town. It's a great place to live.'

'Oh, yes,' I said as we got into my jeep and began to laugh. 'You're right about that. It's the best.'

24

'That is the tastiest ice-cream sundae I've ever eaten,' Nan said. 'And that's saying something considering my age.'

We were sitting out the front of Sandy's Diner. It was late afternoon, and after completing my article about Vivian Shelly and Edwina Parkridge's deaths, I decided to take the day off.

'They're hard to beat.' I reached down and patted Trixie. 'Although I'm so full, I doubt I'll ever eat again.'

The day had turned unexpectedly warm after the unsettled weather of the last week. I was feeling quite satisfied with myself. With work and a bit of luck, I'd helped Todd to put two criminals behind bars.

'So Vivian *was* a fraud,' Nan said. 'That's a shame. It would have been nice if there were something in it. I probably did imagine those times when I've felt Frank's presence.'

The disappointment in her voice gave me pause. 'Well,' I said carefully. 'Tony Hall said she really had powers. I suppose we'll never know for sure. But she said something that bears thinking about. The veil between life and death is thin.' I thought. 'Maybe it's so thin that sometimes we *can* see through it.'

'You could be right.' Nan sighed. 'You know, Rosie, I love Dave, but I still miss your grandfather.'

I raised an eyebrow. 'You *love* Dave? I didn't know that.'

Nan chuckled. 'You thought he was just a toy boy? I suppose that's the great thing about love. There's always room for more of it: giving and getting.' Her eyes narrowed on the beach. 'Talking about love...'

I followed her gaze. Todd and Yvonne were walking along the beach. They weren't hand in hand, but they were *very* close. My heart missed a beat as my throat constricted. I couldn't watch, so I looked down. A shadow fell across the table.

'Rosie?'

'Duncan!' I smiled. 'What a surprise!'

'Hello.' He glanced at Nan. 'This must be your beautiful mother.'

'Grandmother!' Nan snorted.

'I don't believe it!'

'Believe it, hot stuff!'

Laughing, Nan glanced at her watch and said she had to get moving. After giving me a none-too-obvious wink, she disappeared down the footpath as Duncan settled into the seat beside me.

'Don't mind Nan,' I said. 'She's as subtle as a sledgehammer. Now I've got to ask, how did you go with your audition?'

'What can I say? *O, what a rogue and peasant slave am I!* You're looking at the next Hamlet!'

'Woohoo!' I cheered and felt another little skip of my heart as I realised what it meant. 'So we're losing you from Cape Carson?'

'For a while.' His eyes met mine. 'Although, it's only a six-week season. I'll be back before you know it.'

'Great.'

I didn't know what to say, and Duncan seemed equally tongue-tied.

'Well,' he said, drawing the word out. 'I wanted to drop by and let you know. Hopefully, I'll see you when I return.'

'Great. I'd like that.'

My eyes met his.

Goodness, I thought. *He's going to kiss me.*

But that would be silly because he barely knew me, and I barely knew—

Duncan kissed me.

His lips were soft on mine and had a faintly salty taste. I was worried that people would see us and, at the same time, I didn't care. All there was for a few seconds was a connection. A timeless thing that I could cherish and hold and keep for myself. Something special. Then he pulled away, gave a bashful smile, and stood.

'Rosie Ryan,' he said. 'I'll see you later.'

'See you then.'

He gave a short nod and headed down the footpath. I watched him grow smaller and smaller until he was gone from view.

Trixie barked.

She was ready for a walk, and so was I.

'Yeah,' I said, standing. 'Life's complicated.'

But as I strolled down Percy Street, I didn't mind one little bit.

But the adventure doesn't end here!

Catch Rosie's next mystery in:

Pizza, Pugs and Murder!

ABOUT THE AUTHOR

Darrell Pitt is a prolific author, with more than two dozen novels in print. Writing for both young and old alike, Darrell's books traverse multiple genres including cozy mysteries, science-fiction and adventure stories. A proud resident of Melbourne, Australia, Darrell shares his home with his wife and says he owns too many books (as if such a thing were possible!)

His literary journey began with a passion for crafting short stories in his youth, eventually evolving into full-length novels. Among his accolades, "A Toaster on Mars" earned a prestigious spot on the shortlist for the 2017 Russell Prize, showcasing Darrell's unique brand of humour. His novel, "The Firebird Mystery", received commendation from The Children's Book Council of Australia as a Notable book in 2015.

Darrell's Teen Superhero series has garnered widespread acclaim, while his Rosie Ryan books are a series of delightful mysteries set in a distinctly Australian environment. Among the books he's currently working on are a tech-thriller, a time-travel novel, and a mystery book set in 1960's Victoria.